THE GIFT OF CHRISTMAS

This Large Print Book carries the
Seal of Approval of N.A.V.H.

THE GIFT OF CHRISTMAS

CHRISTMAS

DEBBIE MACOMBER

THORNDIKE PRESS

A part of Gale, Cengage Learning

GALE
CENGAGE Learning·

Detroit • New York • San Francisco • New Haven, Conn • Waterville, Maine • London

GALE
CENGAGE Learning

LIBRARY OF CONGRESS CATALOGING-IN-PUBLICATION DATA

Macomber, Debbie.
    The Gift of Christmas / By Debbie Macomber. — Large Print edition.
      pages cm. — (Thorndike Press Large Print Romance)
    ISBN 978-1-4104-6547-4 (hardcover) — ISBN 1-4104-6547-0 (hardcover) 1.
Christmas stories. 2. Large type books. I. Title.
PS3563.A2364G54 2013
813'.54—dc23   2013037319

Published in 2013 by arrangement with Harlequin Books S.A.

Printed in Mexico
1 2 3 4 5 6 7 17 16 15 14 13

To Rachel Hauck, Roxanne St. Claire,
Virelle Kidder and Martha Powers,
my Florida sisters.

CHAPTER 1

Ashley Robbins clenched her hands together as she sat in a plush velvet chair ten stories up in a Seattle high-rise. The cashier's check to Cooper Masters was in her purse. Rather than mail him the money, Ashley had impulsively decided to deliver it herself.

People moved about her, in and out of doors, as she thoughtfully watched their actions. Curious glances darted her way. She had never been one to blend into the background. Over the years she'd wondered if it was the striking ash blond hair that attracted attention, or her outrageous choice of clothes. Today, however, since she was meeting Cooper, she'd dressed conservatively. Never shy, she was a hit in the classroom, using techniques that had others shaking their heads in wonder. But no one doubted that she was the most popular teacher at John Knox Christian High School. Cooper had made that possible. No one knew he had loaned her the money to complete her studies. Not even Claudia, her best friend and Cooper's niece.

Ashley and Cooper were the godparents to John, Claudia's older boy. Being linked to Cooper had pleased Ashley more than her friend suspected. She'd been secretly in love with him since she was sixteen. It amazed her that no one had guessed during those ten years, least of all Cooper.

"Mr. Masters will see you now," his receptionist informed her.

Ashley smiled her appreciation and followed the attractive woman through the heavy oak door.

"Ashley." Cooper stood and strode to the front of his desk. "What a pleasant surprise."

"Hello, Cooper." He'd changed over the last six months since she'd seen him. Streaks of silver ran through his hair, and tiny lines fanned out from his eyes. But it would take more than years to disguise his strongly marked features. He wasn't a compellingly handsome man, not in the traditional sense, but seeing him again stirred familiar feelings of admiration and appreciation for all he'd done for her.

"Sit down, please." He indicated a chair not unlike the one she'd recently vacated. "What can I do for you? Any problems?"

She responded with a slight shake of her head. He had always been generous with her. Deep down, she doubted that there was anything she couldn't ask of this man, although she didn't expect any more favors, and he was probably aware of that.

"Everything's fine." She didn't meet his eyes as she opened the clasp of her purse and took out the check. "I wanted to personally give you this." Extending her arm, she handed him the check. "I owe you so much, it seemed almost rude to put it in the mail." The satisfaction of paying off the loan was secondary to the opportunity of seeing Cooper again. If she'd been honest with herself, she would have admitted she was hungry for the sight of him. After all these months she'd been looking for an excuse.

He glanced at the check and seemed to notice the amount. Two dark brows arched with surprise. "This satisfies the loan," he said thoughtfully. Half turning, he placed the check in the center of the large wooden desk. "Your mother tells me you've taken a second job?" The intonation in his voice made the statement a question.

"You see her more often than I do," she said in an attempt to evade the question. Her mother had been the Masters' cook and

9

housekeeper from the time Ashley was a child.

He regarded her steadily, and although she could read no emotion in his eyes, she felt his irritation. "Was it necessary to pay this off as quickly as possible?"

"Fast? I've owed you this money for over four years." She laughed lightly. Someone had once told her that her laugh was one of the most appealing things about her. Sweet, gentle, melodic. She chanced a look at Cooper, whose cool dark eyes revealed nothing.

"I didn't care if you ever paid me back. I certainly didn't expect you'd half kill yourself to return it."

The displeasure in his voice surprised her. Taken aback, she watched as he stalked to the far corner of the office, putting as much distance between them as possible. Was it pride that had driven her to pay him back as quickly as possible? Maybe, but she doubted it. The loan to finish her schooling had been the answer to long, difficult prayers. From the time she'd been accepted into the University of Washington, she had attended on faith. Faith that God would supply the money for books and tuition. Faith that if God wanted her to obtain her teaching degree, then He would meet her needs. And He had. In the beginning things had worked well. She roomed with Claudia and managed two part-time jobs. But when Claudia and Seth got married, she was forced to find other accommodations, which quickly drained her funds. Cooper's offer had been completely unexpected. The loan had come at a time when she'd been hopeless and had been preparing to withdraw from classes. They'd never discussed terms, but surely he'd known she intended to repay him.

A tentative smile brushed her lips. She'd thought he would be pleased. His reaction amazed her. She attempted to keep her voice level as she assured him, "It was the honorable thing to do."

"But it wasn't necessary," he answered, turning back to her.

Again she experienced the familiar twinge of awareness that only Cooper Masters was capable of stirring within her.

"It was for me," she countered quickly.

"It wasn't necessary," he repeated in a flat tone.

Ashley released a slow breath. "We could go on like this all day. I didn't mean to offend you, I only came here today because I wanted to show my appreciation."

He stared back at her, then slowly nodded. "I understand."

Silence stretched between them.

"Have you heard from Claudia and Seth?" he asked after a while.

Ashley smiled. They had so little in common that whenever they were together that the conversation invariably centered around Claudia and their godson. "The last I heard she said something about coming down for Christmas."

"I hope they do." His intercom buzzed, and he leaned over and pressed a button on the phone. "Yes, Gloria?"

"Mr. Benson is here."

"Thank you."

Taking her cue, Ashley stood. "I won't keep you." Her fingers brushed her wool skirt. She'd been hoping he would notice the new outfit and comment. He hadn't. "Thank you again. I guess you know that I wouldn't have been able to finish school without your help."

"I was wondering . . ." Cooper moved to her side, his look slightly uneasy, as if he was unsure of himself. "I mean, I can understand if you'd rather not."

"Rather not what?" She couldn't remember him ever acting with anything but supreme confidence. In control of himself and every situation.

12

"Have dinner with me. A small celebration for paying off the loan."

"I'd like that very much. Anytime." Her heart soared at the suggestion; she wasn't sure how she managed to keep her voice level.

"Tonight at seven?"

"Wonderful. Should I wear something . . . formal?" It wouldn't hurt to ask, and he hadn't mentioned where he intended they dine.

"Dress comfortably."

"Great."

An hour later Ashley's heart still refused to beat at a normal pace. This was the first time Cooper had asked her out or given any indication he would like to see her socially. The man was difficult to understand, always had been. Even Claudia didn't fully know him; she saw him as dignified, predictable and overly concerned with respectability. In some ways he was, but through the years Ashley had seen past that facade. He might be refined, and sometimes overly proper, but he was a man who'd been forced to take on heavy responsibility at an early age. There had been little time for fun or frivolity in his life. Ashley wanted to be the one to change that. She loved him. Her mother claimed that opposites attract, and after meeting Cooper, Ashley had never doubted the truth of that statement.

Ashley chose to wear her finest designer jeans, knowing she looked good. At five foot nine, she was all legs. Her pink sweatshirt contained a starburst of sequins that extended to the ends of the full length sleeves. Her hair was styled in a casual perm, and soft curls reached her shoulders. Her perfume was a fragrance Cooper had given her the previous Christmas. Although not imaginative, the gift had pleased her immeasurably, even though he hadn't given it to her personally, but to her mother, who'd passed it on. When she'd phoned to thank him, his response had been clipped and vaguely ill-at-ease. Politely, he'd assured her that it was his duty, since they were John's godparents. He'd also told her he'd sent the same fragrance to Claudia. Ashley had hung up the phone feeling deflated. The next time she'd seen him had been in June, when her mother had gone to the hospital for surgery. Cooper had come for a visit at the same time Ashley had arrived. Standing on opposite sides of the bed, her sleeping mother between them, Ashley had hungrily drunk in the sight of him. Their short conversation had been carried on in hushed tones, and after a while they hadn't spoken at all. Afterward he'd had coffee out of a machine, and she'd sipped fruit juice as they sat talking in the waiting area at the end of the corridor. She hadn't seen him again until today.

Over the months she had dated several men, and she'd recently been seeing Dennis Webb, another teacher, on a steady basis. But no one had ever attracted her the way Cooper did. Whenever a pensive mood overtook her, she recognized how pointless that attraction was. Whole universes stretched between them, both social and economic. For Ashley, loving Cooper Masters was as impossible as understanding income tax forms.

The doorbell chimed precisely at seven. Claudia had claimed that she could set her watch by Cooper. If he said seven, he would arrive exactly at seven.

A sense of panic filled Ashley as she glanced at her wristwatch. It couldn't possibly be that time already, could it? With one red cowboy boot on and the other lying on the carpet, she looked around frantically. The laundry still hadn't been put away. Quickly she hobbled across the floor and shoved the basket full of folded clean clothes into the entryway closet, then closed the door with her back as she conducted a sweeping inspection of the apartment. Expelling a calming sigh, she forced herself to smile casually as she opened the door.

He greeted her with a warm look, that gradually faded as he handed her a florist's box.

To Cooper, apparently informal meant a three-piece suit and flowers. Glancing down at her jeans and sweatshirt, one cowboy boot on, the other missing, she smiled weakly and felt wretched. "Thank you." She took the small white box. "Sit down, please." Hurrying ahead of him, she fluffed up the pillows at the end of the sofa, then hugged one to her stomach. "I'm running a little late tonight. If you'll give me a few minutes I'll change clothes."

"You look fine just the way you are," he murmured, glancing at his watch.

What he was really saying, she realized, was that they would be late for their reservation if she took the time to change clothes. After glancing down at the hot pink sweatshirt, she raised her gaze to meet his. "You're sure? It'll only take a minute."

His nod seemed determined. Self-conscious, embarrassed and angry with herself, Ashley sat at the opposite end of the sofa and slipped her foot into the other boot. After tucking in her denim pant leg, she sat up and reached for the florist's box. A lovely white orchid was nestled in a bed of sheer green paper. A gasp of pleasure escaped her.

"Oh, Cooper," she murmured, feeling close to tears. No one had ever given her an orchid. "Thank you."

"Since I didn't know the color of your dress . . ." He paused to correct himself. ". . . your outfit . . . this seemed appropriate." He remained standing, studying her. "It's the type women wear on their wrist."

As Ashley lifted the orchid from the box, its gentle fragrance drifted pleasantly to her. "I'm always having to thank you, Cooper. You've been very good to me."

He dismissed her appreciation with a hard shake of his head. "Nonsense."

She knew that further discussion would only embarrass them both. Standing, she glanced at the closet door, knowing nothing would induce her to open it and expose her folded underwear to Cooper. "I'll get my purse and we can go."

"You might want to wear a coat," he suggested. "I heard something about the possibility of snow over the radio this afternoon."

"Yes, of course." If he remained standing exactly as he was, she might be able to open the door just enough to slip her hand in and jerk her faux fur jacket off the hanger. Somehow she managed it. Turning, she noted that Cooper was regarding her curiously. Rather than fabricate a wild excuse about why she couldn't open the closet all the way, she decided to say nothing.

He took the coat from her grasp, holding it open for her to slip her arms into the sleeves. It seemed as if his hands lingered longer than necessary on her shoulders, but it could have been her imagination. He had never been one to display affection openly.

"Where are we going?" she asked, and her voice trembled slightly, affected by even the most impersonal touch.

"I chose an Italian restaurant not far from here. I hope that suits you."

"Sounds delicious. I love Italian food." Her tastes in food were wide and varied, but it wouldn't have mattered. If he had suggested hot dogs, she would have been thrilled. The idea of Cooper eating anything with his fingers produced a quivering smile. If he noticed it, he said nothing.

Cooper parked outside the small, family-owned restaurant and came around to her side of the car, opening the door for her. It was apparent when they were seated that he had never been there before. The thought flashed through her mind that he didn't want to be seen with her where he might be recognized. But she quickly dismissed the idea. If he didn't want to be with her, then he wouldn't have asked her out. Those thoughts were unworthy of Cooper, who had always been good to her.

"Is everything all right?" As he stared across the table at her, a frown drew his brows together.

"Yes, of course." She looked down at her menu, guiltily forcing a smile on her face. "I wonder how long it'll be before we know if Claudia will be coming for Christmas," she said, hoping to resume the even flow of conversation.

"Time's getting close. I imagine we'll know soon."

Thanksgiving was the following weekend, but Christmas displays were already up in stores; some had shown up as early as Halloween. Doubtless Seth and Claudia would let them know by the end of next week. The prospect of sharing the holiday with her friend — and therefore Cooper — produced a glow of happiness inside Ashley.

The waiter took their order, then promptly delivered their fresh green salads.

"It's been exceptionally chilly for this time of the year," Cooper commented, lifting his fork, his gaze centered on his plate.

Ashley thought it was a sad commentary that their only common ground consisted of Claudia and the weather. "Yes, it has." She looked up to note that a veiled look had come over his features. Perhaps he was thinking the same thing.

The conversation during dinner seemed stiff and strained to her. Cooper asked her about school and politely inquired if she liked teaching. In return she asked him about the business supply operation he owned and was surprised to learn how much it had grown over the past few years. The knowledge should have pleased her, but instead it only served to remind her that he was a rich man and she was still struggling financially.

When they stepped out of the restaurant, she was pleased to discover that it was snowing.

"Oh, Cooper, look!" she cried with delight. "I love it when it snows. Let's go for a walk." She couldn't keep the excitement out of her voice. "There's something magical about walking in the falling snow."

"Are you sure that's what you want?" He glanced at the thin layer of white powder that covered the ground, then he looked up, his expression odd as his eyes searched hers.

"I'd forgotten, you'll have to drive back in this stuff. Maybe it wouldn't be such a good idea," she commented, unable to hide her disappointment.

His hand cupped her elbow, bringing her near, and when she slipped on the slick sidewalk he quickly placed his arm around her waist, preventing her from falling. He left his arm there, holding her protectively close to his side. Her spirits soared at being linked this way with Cooper.

"Where would you like to walk?" An indiscernible expression clouded his eyes.

"There's a marina a couple of blocks from here, and I love to watch the snow fall on the water, but if you'd rather not, I understand."

"By all means, let's go to the marina." The smile he gave her was the first genuine one she'd witnessed the entire evening.

"Doesn't this make you want to sing?" she asked, and started to hum "White Christmas" even before he could answer.

"No," he said, and chuckled. "It makes me want to sit in front of a roaring fireplace with a warm drink."

She clucked and pressed her lips together to keep from laughing.

"What was that all about?"

"What?" she asked, feigning ignorance.

"That silly little noise you just made."

"If you must know, I don't think you've done anything impulsive or daring in your entire life, Cooper Masters." She said it all in one giant breath, then watched as a shocked look came over his face.

"Of course I have," he insisted righteously.

"Then I dare you to do something right now."

"What?" He looked unsure.

"Make a snowball and throw it at me," she demanded. Breaking from his hold, she ran a few steps ahead of him. "Bet you can't do it," she taunted, and waved her hands at him.

With marked determination, Cooper stuffed his hands inside his coat pockets. "This is silly."

"It's supposed to be crazy, remember?" she chided him softly.

"But it's not right for a man to throw snowballs at a woman."

"Will this make things easier for you?" she shouted, bending over to scoop up a handful of snow. With an accuracy that astonished her, she threw a snowball that hit him directly in the middle of his chest. If she was surprised, the horrified look on Cooper's face sent her into peals of laughter. Losing her balance on the ice-slickened sidewalk, she went sprawling to the cement with an undignified plop.

"That's what you get for hurling snow at courteous gentlemen," Cooper called once he was sure she wasn't hurt. As he advanced toward her, he shifted a tightly packed snowball from one hand to the other.

"Cooper, you wouldn't — would you?" She gave him her most defenseless look, batting her eyelashes. "Here, help me up." She extended a hand to him, which he ignored.

A wicked gleam flashed from the dark depths of his eyes. "I thought you said I never did anything crazy or daring?"

"You wouldn't!" Her voice trembled with laughter as she struggled to stand up.

"You're right, I wouldn't," he murmured, dropping the snowball and reaching for her. Surprise rocked her as he pulled her into his arms. He hesitated momentarily, as if expecting her to protest. When she didn't, he gently brushed the hair from her temple and just as softly pressed his mouth over hers. The kiss should have been tender, but the moment their lips met it became hungry and needy. The effect was jarring, as if a bolt of awareness were flashing through them. They broke apart, shocked and breathless. The oxygen was trapped in her lungs, making it impossible to breathe.

"Did I hurt you?" he asked, his voice thick with concern.

A shake of her head was all she could manage. "Cooper?" Her voice was a mere whisper. "Would you mind doing that again?"

"Now?"

She nodded.

"Here?"

Again she nodded.

He pulled her back into his embrace, his eyes drinking deeply from hers. This time the kiss was gentle, as if he, too, needed to test these sensations. Lost in the swirling awareness, Ashley felt as if he had touched the deep inner part of her being. For years she had dreamed of this moment, wondered what effect his touch would have on her. Now she knew. She felt a free-flowing happiness steal over her. He had taken her heart and touched her spirit. When he entwined his fingers in the curling length of her hair, she pressed her head against his shoulder and breathed in deeply. A soft smile lifted her lips at the sound of his furiously pounding heart.

"This is crazy," he murmured hoarsely.

"No," she swiftly countered. "This is wonderful."

Carefully he relaxed his hold, easing her

from his embrace. His features were un-naturally pale as he smoothed the hair at the side of his head with an impatient move-ment. "I'm too old for you." His mouth had thinned, and his look was remote.

Her bubble of happy contentment burst; he regretted kissing her. What had been so wonderful for her was a source of embar-rassment for him. "I dared you to do some-thing impulsive, remember?" she said with forced gaiety. "It doesn't mean anything. I've been kissed before. It happens all the time."

"I'm sure it does," he replied stiffly. His gaze moved pointedly to his watch. "I think it would be best if I took you home now. Perhaps we could see the marina another time."

"Sure."

His touch was impersonal as they strolled purposefully back toward the restaurant parking lot. To hide her discomfort, Ashley began to hum Christmas music again.

"Rushing the season a bit, aren't you?"

She concentrated on moving one foot in front of the other. "I suppose. But the snow makes it feel like Christmas. Christ wouldn't mind if we celebrated His birth every day of the year."

"The shopping malls would love it if we

did," he remarked cynically.

"You're speaking of the commercial aspect of the holiday, I'm talking about the spiritual one."

Cooper didn't comment. In fact, neither one of them spoke until he pulled up to the curb in front of her apartment building.

"Would you like to come in and warm up? It would only take a minute to heat up some cocoa." Although the offer was sincere, she knew he wouldn't accept.

"Perhaps another time."

There wouldn't be another time. He wouldn't ask her out again; the whole evening had been a fiasco. Cooper Masters was a powerful, influential man, whereas she was a high school English Lit teacher.

"You'll let me know if you hear anything from Seth and Claudia?"

"Of course."

He came around to her side of the car, opening the door. "You don't need to walk me all the way to my door," she mumbled miserably.

"There's every need." Although his voice was level, she could tell he was determined to live up to what he felt a gentleman should be.

She didn't argue when he took the keys out of her hand and opened the door of her first-floor apartment for her. "Thank you," she murmured. "The evening was . . ."

"Crazy," he finished for her.

Wonderful, her mind insisted in return. Afraid of what her eyes would reveal, she lowered her head and her blond curls fell forward, wreathing her face. "Crazy," she repeated.

A finger placed under her chin lifted her eyes to his. His were dark and unreadable, hers soft and shining. Slowly his hand moved to caress the soft, smooth skin of her cheek. The gentle caress sent the blood pulsing through her veins, flushing her face with telltale color.

"If ever you're in trouble or need someone, I want you to contact me."

Although he had never verbally said as much, she had always been aware that she could go to him if ever she needed help.

"I will." Her voice sounded irritatingly weak.

"I want you to promise me." He unbuttoned his coat pocket and took out a business card. Using the door as a support, he wrote down a phone number. "You can reach me here any time of the day."

"I'm not going to trouble you with —"

"Promise me, Ashley."

He was so serious, his look demanding.

27

"Okay," she agreed, accepting the card. "But why?"

A long moment passed before he answered her. "I have a vested interest in you," he said, and shrugged, the indifferent gesture contradicting his words. "Besides, I'd hate to have anything happen to Johnny's godmother."

"Nothing's going to happen to me."

"In case it does, I want you to know I'll always be there."

The business card seemed to sear her hand. In his own way, Cooper cared about her. "Thank you." Impulsively, she raised two fingers to her lips, then brushed them across his mouth. His hand stopped hers, gripping her wrist; his look branded her. Slowly he lowered his mouth to hers in a gentle, sweet kiss.

"Good night, Ashley."

"Good night." Standing in the open doorway, she watched until he drove into the dark night. A solitary figure illuminated by the falling snow.

Expelling her breath in a long quivering sigh, she tucked the card in her purse. Why did she have to love Cooper Masters? Why couldn't she feel for Webb what she did for Cooper? Webb was nice and almost as unpredictable as she was. Maybe that was why they got along so well. Yet it was Cooper who occupied her thoughts. Cooper who made her heart sing. Cooper who filled her dreams. The time had come to wake up and face reality. She was at the age when she should start thinking about marriage and a family, because she definitely wanted children. Cooper wasn't going to be interested in someone like her. He might care about her, even feel some affection for her, but she wasn't the type of woman he would ever ask to be his wife.

Troubled and confused, Ashley made herself a cup of cocoa and sat on the sofa, her feet tucked under the cushion next to her. Things had been so easy for her friends, even Claudia. They met someone, fell in love, got married and started a family. Maybe God had decided He didn't want her to marry. The thought seemed intolerable, but she had learned long ago not to second-guess her heavenly Father. She'd given Him her life, her will, even Cooper's safekeeping. Now she had to learn to trust.

She rinsed out the cup, placed it in the kitchen sink and turned out the lights. Her eyes fell on her purse, hanging on the closet doorknob. She wondered if the day might come when she would need to use the card, not that she intended to.

■ ■ ■ ■

That same thought ran through her mind several days later when the police officer directed her to the phone. She didn't want to contact Cooper, so she'd tried phoning her family first, hoping she would catch her father at home. But there had been no answer.

"Is there anyone else, Miss?" the tall, uniformed man asked.

"Yes," she answered tightly, opening her purse and taking out the card. Her fingers actually trembled as she dialed the number.

"Cooper Masters."

As she suspected, he'd given her his private cell number. "Oh, hi . . . it's Ashley."

"Ashley." His voice carried clearly over the line. "What's wrong?"

"It isn't an emergency or anything," she began, feeling incredibly silly. "I mean, I don't think they'll keep me."

"Ashley," he heaved her name on an angry sigh. "What's going on?"

"It's a long story."

"All right, tell me where you are. I'll come to you, and then we'll straighten everything out."

She hesitated, swallowing past the lump forming in her throat. "I'm in jail."

CHAPTER 2

"Jail!" Cooper's voice boomed over the line. "I'll be there in ten minutes."

"But, Cooper, Kent's a good thirty minutes from downtown Seattle."

"Kent?" The anger in his voice was barely controlled.

"If you're going to get so mad . . ." Ashley let the rest of the sentence fade, realizing that the phone line had already been disconnected.

Casting a glance at the police officer beside her, she gave him a wary smile. "A friend's coming."

A smile quivered at one corner of the older man's mouth. "I heard." Looking away, he asked, "Would you like a cup of coffee while you wait?"

"No thanks."

Ashley heard Cooper's voice several minutes before she saw him. By the time he was brought into the area where she was waiting, there wasn't a person in the entire police station who hadn't heard him. She had always known him to be a calm, discreet person. That he would react this way to a minor misunderstanding shocked her. Although . . . a lot of things about Cooper had surprised her lately. She was standing, her face devoid of color, when he was escorted into the room.

"Can you tell me what's going on here?" he demanded.

His look did little to encourage confidences; she swallowed tightly and waved her hand helplessly. "Well, apparently someone took the license plate off Milligan."

"Who the heck . . . ?" He paused and took a deep, calming breath. "Who's Milligan?"

"Not who," she corrected, "but what. Milligan's my moped. I parked it outside the Mexican restaurant where I work odd hours, and someone apparently took off with my license plate."

"That isn't any reason to arrest you!" he shouted.

"They haven't arrested me!" she yelled in return, and was humiliated when her voice cracked and wavered. "And if you won't quit shouting at me, then you can just leave."

Raking his fingers roughly through his

hair, Cooper stalked to the other side of the room. His mouth was tightly pinched, and he said nothing for several long moments. "All right, let's try this again," he replied in a deceivingly soft tone. "Start at the beginning, and tell me everything."

"There's not much to tell. Someone took the license plate, and, since I don't have the registration on me, the police need some evidence that I own the bike. I haven't been arrested or anything. In fact, they've been very nice." In nervous reaction she looped a long strand of curly hair around her ear. "All I need for you to do is go to my apartment and bring back the registration for Milligan. Then I'll be free to leave." She opened her purse and took out her key ring, then extracted the key to the apartment. "Here," she said, handing it to him. "The registration's in the kitchen, in the silverware drawer, stuck under the aluminum foil. I keep all my important papers there."

If he thought her record storage system was a bit unusual, he said nothing.

"There's a lawyer on his way here, I'll leave word at the front desk for him." Without another word, he turned and left the room.

Within twenty minutes she heard him talking to the officer who had offered her the coffee. A few moments later they both entered the waiting area.

"You're free to go," the policeman explained. "Although I'm afraid we can't let you drive the moped until you have a new license plate."

Before she could protest Cooper inserted, "No need to worry. I've already made arrangements for the bike to be picked up." He turned and directed his words to Ashley. "It'll be delivered to your place sometime tomorrow afternoon."

Rather than argue, Ashley mutely agreed.

"If you're ready, I'll take you home," Cooper said.

Shoving her knit cap onto her head, she stood and swung her backpack over her shoulder, then gave the kind officer a polite smile. She wasn't pleased with the way things were working out. If she didn't have Milligan, she would have to take a series of busses to and from work, with a long trek between stops. Surely something could be done to enable her to ride her moped until she could replace the plate. One look from Cooper discouraged her from asking.

His hand cupped her elbow as they walked to the parking lot. Her attention was centered on the scenery outside the car window as they crossed the Green River and connected with the freeway. Wordlessly, he took the first exit and a couple of minutes later pulled into the parking lot to her apartment building.

He turned off the engine, then called his office. "Gloria, cancel the rest of my appointments for today," he said stiffly, his voice clipped and abrupt. Without waiting for a confirmation, he promptly ended the call, and then turned to Ashley. "Invite me in for coffee."

Her heart lodged someplace near her throat. "Yes, of course." She didn't wait for him to come around to her side of the car and let herself out. He gave her a disapproving look as they met in front of the vehicle. He opened the apartment door and returned the key to her. She placed it back on the key ring and took off her jacket, carelessly tossing it across the top of the sofa. He removed his black overcoat and neatly folded it over the back of the chair opposite the sofa.

"I'll put on the coffee." She moved into the kitchen, pouring water into the small, five-cup pot. She could hear Cooper agitatedly pacing the floor behind her.

"Why are you so angry with me?" she asked. She couldn't look at him, not when he was so obviously furious with her. "I couldn't help it if someone stole my license plate. I never should have phoned you, I'm sorry I did."

"I'm not mad at you," he stormed. "I'm angry that you were put through that ordeal, that you were treated like a criminal, that . . ." He left the rest unsaid.

"It's not the policeman's fault. He was only doing his job," she tried to explain, still not facing him. Her fingers trembled as she added the grounds to the pot, placed the lid on top and set it to brew.

A large masculine hand landed on her shoulder, and she had to fight not to lay her cheek on it. A subtle pressure turned her around. With both hands behind her, she gripped the oven door for support. Slowly she raised her eyes to meet his. She was surprised at the tenderness she saw in the dark depths of his gaze, which seemed to be centered on her mouth. Nervously she moistened her dry lips with the tip of her tongue. She hadn't meant to be provocative, but when Cooper softly groaned she realized what she'd done. When he reached for her, she went willingly into his embrace.

He held her against him, breathing in deeply as he buried his face in the curve of her neck. His hands roamed her back, arching her as close as humanly possible. Ashley molded herself to him, savoring the light scent of musk and man; she longed for him to kiss her. She silently pleaded with him to throw common sense to the wind and crush his mouth over hers. Just being held by him was more happiness than she'd ever hoped to experience. Happiness and torment all rolled into one. An embrace, a light caress, a longing look, could never satisfy her, not when she wanted so much more. Gently he kissed the crown of her head and released her. She wanted to cry with disappointment.

The coffee had begun to perk, and to disguise her emotions, Ashley turned and reached for two cups, waiting for the pot to finish before pouring.

While she dealt with the coffee, Cooper sat in the living room waiting for her. He stood when she entered, taking one cup from her hand.

"I'm sorry, Ashley," he said, his eyes probing hers.

He didn't need to elaborate. He was sorry for his anger, sorry he'd overreacted in the police station, but mostly he regretted throwing aside his self-control and taking her in his arms.

Unable to verbally acknowledge his apology she simply shook her head, letting him know that she understood what he was saying.

"So you work at a Mexican restaurant?" he asked, after taking a sip from the steaming cup.

She wasn't fooled by the veiled interest. He'd commented on the fact she'd taken a second job once before, and he hadn't been pleased then.

"I only work odd hours, less now that I've paid off the loan," she answered, her finger making lazy loops around the rim of her cup.

He pinched his mouth tightly shut, and she recognized that he was biting back words. She wondered how he managed in business confrontations when she found him so easy to read.

Taking another sip of coffee, he stood and moved into the kitchen to put the half-full cup into the sink. "I should go."

She followed his movements. "I haven't thanked you. I . . . I don't know what I would have done if you hadn't come."

Her appreciation seemed to embarrass him, because his mouth thinned. He lifted his coat off the back of the chair. "I said I wanted you to call me if you needed help. I'm glad you did."

She walked him to the door. "How'd you

get to Kent so fast?" Asking him questions helped delay the time when he would leave. "I was already in the car when you phoned. It was simply a matter of heading in the right direction."

"Oh," she said in a small voice. "I apologize if I inconvenienced you."

"You didn't," he returned gruffly. His eyes met hers then, and again she found herself drowning in those dark depths.

Clenching her hands at her sides, she gave him a falsely cheerful smile. "Thanks again, Cooper. God go with you."

He turned. "And you," he murmured, surprising her.

"Have a nice Thanksgiving."

"I'm sure I will. Are you spending the day with your family?"

"Yes, Mom's making her famous turkey stuffing, and Jeff and his wife, Marsha, are coming." Jeff was her younger brother. John, the youngest Robbins, was working in Spokane and had decided not to make the long drive over the Cascade Mountains in uncertain weather.

Cooper didn't elaborate on his own plans for the holiday, and she didn't ask. "Goodbye, and thanks again."

"Goodbye, Ashley."

As she watched him walk away, she had

the strongest desire to blow him a kiss. Immediately she quelled the impulse, but she couldn't help feeling disappointed and frustrated. Closing the front door, she leaned against it and breathed in deeply. She was filling her head with fanciful dreams if she dared to hope Cooper would ever come to love her. Wasting her time and her life. But her heart refused to listen.

As Cooper promised, her moped was delivered safely to her apartment the following afternoon. Webb drove her home from school, and once she dropped off her things, he took her to the Department of Motor Vehicles, where she applied for new license plates. Granted a temporary plate, she was relieved to learn she could now ride Milligan. The moped might not be much, but it got her where she needed to go in the most economical way.

Webb was tall and thin, his facial features almost gaunt, but he was one of the nicest people Ashley had ever known. When he dropped her off at her apartment, she invited him inside. He accepted with a smile.

"Got plans for the weekend?" he asked over a cup of cocoa.

She shrugged. "Not really. I wanted to do

some Christmas shopping, but I dread fighting the crowds."

"Want to go skiing Saturday afternoon? I understand the slopes are open."

"I didn't know you skied?" Ashley questioned, her eyes twinkling.

"I don't," Webb confirmed. "I thought you'd teach me."

"Forget that, buddy. You can take lessons like everyone else, then we'll talk about skiing," she said with a laugh. "You could invite me to dinner instead," she suggested hopefully.

"Fine, what are you cooking?"

"Leftovers."

"I'll bring the egg nog," he said with a sly grin.

"Honestly, Webb, how do you do it?" she asked, laughing.

"Do what?"

"Invite me out to dinner, and I end up cooking?"

"It's all in the wrist, all in the wrist," he told her, flexing his hand, looking smug.

Thinking about their conversation later, she couldn't help laughing. Webb was a fun person, but what she felt for Cooper was exciting and intense and couldn't compare with the friendship she shared with her coworker.

With Cooper she felt vulnerable in a way that couldn't be explained. But then she was in love with Cooper Masters, and that was simply pointless.

Disturbed by her thoughts, she went to change clothes. As part of her preparation for the coming holidays and the extra calories she would consume, she had started to work out. Following the instructions on the DVD she'd purchased, she practiced a routine that used Christian music for an aerobic dancercise program. Dressed in purple satin shorts, pink leg-warmers and a gray T-shirt, she placed her hands on her hips in the middle of the living room and waited for the warm-up instructions. Just as she completed the first round of exercises, the doorbell rang.

She paused, and with her breath deep and ragged, she turned off the player and checked the peep hole in the door. She wasn't expecting anyone. To her horror, she saw it was Cooper.

The doorbell buzzed again, and for a fleeting second she was tempted to let him think she wasn't home, but overriding her embarrassment at having him see her dressed in shorts and a T-shirt was her desire to know why he'd come.

"Hello," she said as she opened the door.

He walked into the apartment, his brow marred by a puzzled frown as he glanced at her. "Maybe I should come back later."

"Nonsense," she mumbled, dismissing the suggestion. She grabbed a towel to wipe the perspiration from her face. "I was just doing some aerobics. Care to join me?"

"No thanks." The corners of his mouth formed deep grooves as he suppressed a smile. "But don't let me stop you."

His attempt at humor amazed her. It was the first time she could remember him bantering with her — or anyone. "I think I'll skip the rest of the program," she said and laughed.

"Is that coffee I smell?" he asked as he sat on the edge of the sofa.

"No, cocoa. Want some? If you want coffee, though, it'd only take me a minute to brew a pot."

He shook his head.

Looping the towel around her neck, she sat Indian style opposite him. Her face was glowing and red from the exertion, and she noted the way Cooper couldn't keep his eyes off her. Her heart was pounding fiercely, but she wasn't sure if it was the effects of seeing him again or the aerobics.

For a long moment silence filled the room.

"Did you get Madigan back?" he eventually asked.

"Milligan," she corrected.

"How'd you happen to name a moped Milligan?"

"It was the salesman's name. We went out a couple of times afterward, and I couldn't think of the bike without thinking of Milligan, so I started calling it by his name."

Cooper's mouth narrowed slightly. "What do you do when it rains?"

"Wear rain gear," she returned casually. "It's a bit of a hassle, but I don't mind." Why was he so curious about Milligan? Certainly he'd known — or at least known of — someone who rode a moped before now?

"They're not the safest thing around, are they?"

"I suppose not, but I'm careful." This line of questioning was beginning to rankle. "Why all the curiosity?"

Leaning forward, he rested his elbows on his knees, then quickly shifted position, placing his ankle across one knee as if to give a casual impression. "The more I thought about you riding that moped, the more concerned I became. In checking statistics I discovered —"

"Statistics?" she interrupted him. "Hon-

45

estly, Cooper, I'm perfectly safe."

He closed his eyes for a moment in apparent frustration, then opened them again. "I knew this wasn't going to be easy. You're as stubborn as Claudia," he said, and expelled his breath slowly. "I'm going to worry about you riding around on that silly bit of chrome and rubber."

"I've had Milligan for almost two years," she inserted, feeling the color drain from her face.

"Ashley," he said, his gaze lingering on her. "I want you to accept these and promise me you'll use them." He took a set of keys from his pocket and held them out to her.

"What are they?" her voice trembled slightly.

"The keys to a new car. If you don't like the color we can —"

"The keys to a new car?" she echoed in shocked disbelief. "You don't honestly expect me to accept that, do you?"

"No," he acknowledged with a heavy sigh, "knowing you, I didn't think you would. If you insist on paying me —"

"Paying you!" she cried, leaping to her feet. "I just cleared one loan — I'm not about to take on another." Her arms cradling her waist, she paced the floor directly in front of him. "Don't you realize how

46

many enchiladas I had to serve to pay off the last loan? I can't understand you. I can't understand why you'd do something like this."

He inhaled deeply, his look full of trepidation. "I don't want you riding around on a stupid moped and getting yourself killed."

"You know, Cooper, you're beginning to sound like my father. I don't need another parent. I'm a capable twenty-six-year-old woman, not a half-wit teenager. What I ride to work is my prerogative."

"I'm only trying to . . ."

"I know what you're trying to do," she stormed. "Run my life! I have to admit, I was fooled." Her hand flew to her face and she wiped a thin layer of moisture from her brow. "You gave me your phone number and told me to call, but you didn't tell me there were strings attached."

"You're overreacting!" Although he appeared outwardly calm, she knew he was as unsettled as she was. Bright red color was creeping up his neck, but she doubted that he would vent his emotions in front of her.

"I'm not overreacting!" she exclaimed at fever pitch. "You think that because I phoned you, it gives you the right to step into my life. Keep the car, because I assure you I don't need it."

"As you wish," he murmured, his voice tight and controlled. Standing, he returned the keys to his pocket, his expression a stoic mask. "If you'll excuse me, I have an appointment."

"I hope the car isn't in the apartment parking lot, because the manager will have it towed away." The minute the words were out, she regretted having said them.

"It's not," he assured her coldly. Brushing past her, he let himself out, leaving her feeling deflated and depressed. The nerve of the man . . . He seemed to think . . . Her thoughts faded as she felt a hard knot form in her stomach. Now she'd done it, really done it.

"Happy Thanksgiving, Mom." Ashley laid the freshly baked pie on the kitchen countertop and leaned over to kiss her mother on the cheek.

"Hello, sweetheart." Sarah Robbins placed an arm around Ashley's waist and hugged her close. "I'm glad you're early, dear, would you mind peeling the potatoes?"

"Sure, Mom," she agreed, pulling open the kitchen drawer and taking out the peeler. Ashley had hoped for some time to talk to her mother privately. "How's work?" she asked in what she hoped was a casual tone. "Is Mr. Masters cracking the whip?" Her mother would have thought it disrespectful if she'd called Cooper anything but Mr. Masters, but the formal title nearly stuck in her throat.

"Oh, hardly." Sarah wiped the back of her hand across her apron. "He's always been wonderful to work for. I must say, he certainly loves those nephews of his. There are pictures of John and Scott all over that house, and I swear the only reason he moved out of the condominium was so those boys would have a decent yard to play in when they came to visit. That's all he ever talks about." Opening the oven door, she pulled out the rack to baste the turkey with a giblet broth simmering on the top of the stove. "Have you heard from Claudia and Seth?"

Ashley was chewing on a stalk of celery, and she waited until she'd swallowed before answering. "We chat all the time. I'm hoping she'll be here for Christmas."

"That'll please Mr. Masters. I think he needs a bit of cheering up. He's been in the blackest mood the last couple of days."

"He has?" She hoped to disguise her attentiveness. Her family, especially her mother, wouldn't approve of her interest in Cooper. Her feelings for her mother's

49

employer had never been discussed, but she had sensed her mother's subtle disapproval of even their shared role as godparents more than once. In some ways Sarah Robbins and Cooper Masters were a lot alike. Her mother would view it as inappropriate for Ashley to be interested in an important man like Cooper.

"Did you cook a turkey for him this year?"

"No, he said he'd fix himself something, said he didn't want me fussing, when I had a family to tend to," she said on a soft sigh. "He really is the nicest man."

"I think he's wonderful," Ashley agreed absently, without thinking, and colored slightly when she turned to find her mother staring at her with questioning eyes. She was saved from answering any embarrassing questions by her sister-in-law, Marsha, who breezed through the door full of the joy of the season. She was grateful that she and her mother were never alone after that, and soon the meal was on the table.

Everything was delicious, as all her mother's cooking was. As they sat around the table, Ashley's father asked the blessing, then opened the Bible to Psalms and read several praises aloud. After a moment's silence he asked each family member to verbally state one of the blessings they were most thankful for this year. Tears shimmered in Marsha's eyes as she announced that she and Jeff were going to have a baby. The news brought shouts of delight from Ashley's parents. When it came to her turn she thanked God for the rich Christian heritage she had received from her parents and also that she was going to be an aunt at last.

Later, as she helped with the dishes, Ashley's thoughts again drifted to Cooper. Here she was, with a loving family surrounding her, and he was probably alone in his large house. No, she told herself, most likely he was sharing the day with friends or business associates. But she wasn't convinced.

Hounded by constant self-recrimination since their last meeting, she had berated her quick temper a hundred times. He had only been concerned about her safety, and she'd acted as if he'd accosted her.

"Mom," she said and swallowed tightly. "Would you mind if I took a plate of food over to a friend who has to spend the day alone?"

"Of course not, dear, but why didn't you say something earlier? You could have invited them to dinner."

"I wish I'd thought of it," she said.

When she was all set with a large cooler

overflowing with turkey and all the extras, Ashley's father loaned her the family car.

Her heartbeat raced frantically as she pulled into Cooper's driveway in the exclusive Redondo area of south Seattle. She wouldn't blame him if he closed the door on her. He'd purchased the house with the surrounding two acres of prime view property shortly after Claudia had given birth to John. Ashley had never seen the house although her mother had told her about it several times.

Now the large, two-story brick structure loomed before her, elegant and impressive. Adjusting her red beret, she rang the doorbell and waited. Several minutes passed before Cooper answered. He wore a suit, and she couldn't recall ever seeing him look more distinguished.

"Happy Thanksgiving, Cooper," she said with a trembling smile. If he didn't invite her inside, she was afraid she would burst into tears and humiliate them both.

"Ashley." He sounded shocked to see her. "Come in. For heaven's sake you didn't ride that deathtrap moped over here, did you?"

"No." She smiled and cast a glance over her shoulder to the older model car parked in the driveway. "Dad loaned me his car."

"Come in, it's cold, and it looks like rain,"

he offered again. He held out his hand, gesturing her inside.

Ashley didn't need a second invitation. "Here." She handed him the cooler. "I didn't know if you . . ." She hesitated. "Mom sent this along." Might as well jump in with both feet. Being underhanded about anything went against her inherent streak of honesty, but if her mother questioned her later, she would explain then.

Cooper took the cooler into the kitchen. She followed close behind, awestruck by every nook of the impressive home. The kitchen was a study in polished chrome and marble. It looked as clean as a hospital, yet welcoming. That was her mother's gift, she realized.

"Let me fix you something to drink. Coffee okay?" His eyes pinned hers, and she nodded.

After he poured her a mug, she followed him into a room with a fireplace and book-lined walls. His den, she decided. Two dark leather chairs with matching ottomans sat obliquely in front of the fireplace. He took her hat and red wool coat, hung them in a closet and motioned for her to sit in the chair opposite him.

Centering her attention on the steaming coffee, Ashley paused before speaking again.

"I came to apologize."

A movement out of the corner of her eye attracted her gaze, and she watched as Cooper relaxed against the back of the chair.

"Apologize? Whatever for?" he asked.

Her head shot up, and she swallowed the bitter taste in her mouth. He wasn't going to make this easy for her. "I was unforgivably rude the other day, and I have no excuse. You were being thoughtful, and . . ."

He didn't allow her to finish. Instead he gestured with his hand, dismissing her regret. "Nonsense."

Scooting to the very edge of her cushion, she inhaled a quivering breath. "Will you please stop waving at me as though you find my apology amusing?" she said, fighting to keep a grip on her rising irritation. She bolted to her feet and walked to the far side of the room, pretending to examine his collection of books while struggling to keep her composure. Without turning around she mumbled miserably, "I'm sorry, I didn't mean that."

His soft chuckle sounded remarkably close, and when she turned she discovered that only a few inches separated them.

"Oh, Cooper." Her eyes drank in the heady sight of him. "I've felt wretched all week. Please forgive me for the way I acted the other day."

"Have you decided to accept my offer?" The laughter drained from his eyes.

Sadly she shook her head. "Please understand why I can't."

He raked his hands through his hair, ruining the well-groomed effect.

Ashley's finger itched to smooth down the sides, to follow the proud line of his jaw, to touch him. Of its own volition her hand rose halfway to his face before she realized what she was doing.

Their eyes holding one another, Cooper captured her hand and held her motionless. Even his touch had the power to shoot sparks of awareness up her spine. When he raised her fingers to his mouth, his lips gently caressed her knuckles. Trapped in a whirlpool of sensation, she swayed toward him.

Her movement seemed to snap something within him, and he roughly pulled her into his embrace.

"Cooper." His name was a bittersweet sigh that was muffled as his mouth crushed hers. His hold was so tight that for a moment it was difficult to breathe, not that it mattered when she was in his arms.

Automatically, she raised her hands and linked them behind his neck as their mouths strained against one another. It was as if they couldn't get close enough, couldn't give enough. Ashley's lithe frame was flooded with a warm excitement, a glowing happiness that stole over her. A soft, whispering sigh escaped as he moved his face against her hair, brushing against her like a cat seeking contentment.

"Why is it you bring out the —"

The phone interrupted him, the sharp ringing shattering the tender moment. With a low, protesting groan he kissed the tip of her nose and moved across the room to answer the insistent call.

Ashley watched him, her heart swelling with pride and love. Their eyes met, and she noticed a warm light she had never seen in him before.

"Yes," he answered abruptly, then stiffened. "Claudia, this is a surprise."

CHAPTER 3

"Wonderful." Cooper continued speaking into the receiver, his eyes avoiding Ashley's. "Of course you're welcome, you know that. Plan to stay as long as you like."

The conversation lasted several more minutes, but it didn't take Ashley long to realize that Cooper wasn't going to let her friend know she was with him. She couldn't help wondering if she was a source of embarrassment to him. How could he hold her and kiss her one minute, then pretend that she wasn't even there with him the next? The promise of happiness she had savored so briefly in his arms left a bitter aftertaste. He must have sensed her confusion, because he turned away as the conversation with Claudia continued and kept his back to her until it ended a few minutes later.

"That was Claudia and Seth," he told her unnecessarily. "He's got a conference coming up in Seattle the second week of December. They've decided to fly down for that, then stay for the holidays."

He sounded so genuinely pleased that Ashley quickly quelled the spark of hurt. She didn't know why he'd chosen to ignore her, but she was going to put it out of her mind, and she certainly wouldn't ask.

"That's great."

"It is, isn't it?" He moved back to her side, gently easing her into his arms. "This is going to be a wonderful Christmas," he murmured against the softness of her hair.

His voice was like that of an eager child, and it rang a chord of compassion within her. He had taken over his brother's business when he was barely into his twenties. Over the years he had built up the supply operation that extended into ten western states. Claudia had once told her that his goal was to have the business go nationwide. But at what price? she wondered. His health? His personal life? What drove a man like Cooper Masters? she wondered. Could it be the desire for wealth? He was already richer than anyone she knew. Recognition? Yet he was careful to keep a low profile, and from what her mother and Claudia told her, he seemed to jealously guard his privacy. The man was a mystery she might never understand, a puzzle she might never solve.

What did it matter, as long as he held her like this? she asked herself. Her arms around his waist, she laid her head against his solid, muscular chest. The steady beat of his heart sounded in her ear, and she smiled with contentment.

"I feel like doing something crazy," he said, and tipped his head back, laughter dancing in his eyes. "Usually that means taking you in my arms and kissing you like there's no tomorrow."

"I'm game." The urge to wrap her arms around his neck and abandon her pride was almost overwhelming. What pride? her mind echoed. That had been lost long ago where Cooper was concerned.

"Let's go for a walk," he suggested.

Ashley stifled a protest. "It's raining," she warned. A torrential downpour would have been a more accurate description of the turn the weather had taken. She moistened her lips. For once she would have been content to sit in front of the fireplace.

"I'll get us an umbrella," he said, a smile softening the sharp, angular lines of his face.

When he returned, he'd changed clothes and shoes, and was wearing a dark overcoat. A black umbrella dangled from his forearm.

"Ready?" he asked, regarding her expectantly.

He took her red beret and matching wool coat from the closet. He held the coat open for her to slip her arms into the silk-lined sleeves. As he pulled the coat to her shoulders, he paused to gently kiss the slim column of her neck from behind. The tiny kiss shot a tingling awareness over her skin, and she sighed.

"Doesn't this make you want to sing," he teased as they stepped outside. Rain pelted the earth in an angry outburst.

"No." She laughed. "It makes me want to sit in front of a warm fireplace and drink something warm."

Cooper tipped back his head and howled with laughter. She was only echoing his words to her the night it had snowed. It hadn't been that funny. She watched him sheepishly, trying to recall a time she had ever heard him really laugh.

One arm tucked around her waist, he brought her close to his side. "Why is it when I'm with you I want to laugh and sing and behave totally irrationally?"

Wrapping her arm around his waist, she looked up into his sparkling eyes. "I seem to bring out that quality in a lot of people."

He chuckled and opened the umbrella,

which protected them from the worst of the downpour. He led her along a cement walkway that meandered around the property, finally ending at a chain link fence that was built at the top of a bluff that fell sharply into Puget Sound. The night view was spectacular. Ashley could only imagine how much more beautiful it would be during the day. An array of distant lights illuminated the sky and cast their reflective glow into the dark waters of the Sound.

"That must be Vashon Island," she said without realizing she had spoken out loud.

"Yes, and over there's Commencement Bay in Tacoma." He pointed to another section of lights. But his gaze wasn't on the city. Instead she felt it lingering, gently caressing her. When she turned her head, their eyes locked and time came to a screeching halt. Later she wouldn't remember who moved first. But suddenly she was tightly held in his arms, the umbrella carelessly tossed aside as they wrapped one another in a feverish embrace. The kiss that followed was the most beautiful she had ever received, filled with some unnamable emotion, deep, tender, sweet, and all-consuming.

Rain bombarded them, drenching her hair until it hung in wet ringlets. He looked down at her, his breathing uneven and hoarse. Gently he smiled, wiping the moisture from her face. With a laugh, he tugged her hand, and together they ran back to the safety and warmth of the house.

It was the memory of his kiss and that night that sustained Ashley through the long, silent days that followed. Every night she hurried home from work hoping Cooper would contact her in some way. Each day led to bitter disillusionment. When her mother phoned Wednesday afternoon, Ashley already knew what she was going to say.

"Mr. Masters thanked me for the Thanksgiving dinner you brought him. Why didn't you say he was the friend you were going to see?" Her tone hinted of disapproval.

"Because I knew what you would have said if I did," Ashley countered honestly.

"I had no idea you've been seeing Mr. Masters."

"We've only gone out once."

A short, stilted silence followed. "He's too old for you, dear. He's forty, you know."

Closing her eyes, Ashley successfully controlled the desire to argue. "I don't think you need to worry, Mother," she said soothingly. "I doubt that I'll be seeing him again."

"I just don't want to see you get hurt,"

her mother added on a gentler note.

"I know you don't."

They chatted for a few minutes longer and ended the conversation on a happy note, talking about Marsha and the coming baby, her mother's first grandchild.

Replacing the phone, Ashley released a long, slow breath. Cooper's image returned to trouble her again. Everything about him only served as a confirmation of her mother's unspoken warning. He wore expensively tailored suits, his hair was professionally styled, and he seemed to be stamped with an unmistakable look of refinement. Something she would never have. And he was almost fourteen years older than she was, but why should that bother him or her parents when it had never mattered to her? At least she didn't need an explanation for why he hadn't contacted her. After talking to her mother, he had undoubtedly been reminded of their differences. Once again he would shut himself off from her, and who knew how long it would be before she could break through the thick wall of his pride?

Sunday morning during church the pastor lit the first candle of the Advent wreath. Ashley listened attentively as the man of God explained that the first candle represented prophecy. Then he read Scripture from the Old Testament that foretold the birth of a Savior.

Ashley left church feeling more uplifted than she had the entire week. How could she be depressed and miserable at the happiest time of the year? Claudia, Seth and the boys were coming, and Cooper wouldn't be able to avoid seeing her. Perhaps then she could find a way to prove that their obvious differences weren't all that significant.

An email from Claudia was waiting for her after work Monday afternoon. It read:

Ashley,

I'm sorry it's taken me so long to write. I can't believe how busy my boys manage to keep me. I've got some wonderful news! No, I'm not pregnant again, although I don't think Seth would mind. Cooper either, for that matter. He's surprised both of us the way he loves the boys. The good news is that we'll be arriving at Sea/Tac Airport, Saturday, December 12th at 10 A.M. and plan to stay with Cooper through to the first of the year. That first week Seth will be involved in a series of meetings, but the remainder of the time will be the vacation we didn't get the chance to take this summer.

I can't tell you how excited I am to be seeing you again. I've missed you so much. You've always been closer to me than any sister. You'll hardly recognize John. At three, he's taller than most four-year-olds, but then what can we expect, with Seth being almost six-six? There's so much I want to tell you that it seems impossible to put in a letter or speak about over the phone. Promise to block out the holidays on your calendar, because I'm dying to see you again. The Lord's been good to me, and I have so much to tell you.

Scotty just woke from his nap and he never has been one to wake in a happy mood. Take care. I'm counting the days until the 12th.

Love,
Claudia, Seth, John and Scott

Ashley read the message several times. Of course, Claudia didn't realize that she already knew they were coming. Again the hurt washed over her that Cooper had pretended she wasn't there when Claudia had phoned on Thanksgiving Day.

She circled the day on her calendar and stepped back wistfully. When Scott had been born that spring, Cooper had flown up to Nome to spend time with Claudia, Seth and John. Ashley had yet to see the newest Lessinger. Cooper had said it earlier, and now Ashley added her own affirmation. This was going to be the most wonderful Christmas yet.

Ashley's alarm buzzed early the morning of the twelfth. She groaned defiantly until she remembered that she would have to hurry and shower if she was going to meet Claudia's plane as she intended.

A little while later, wearing jeans and a red cable knit sweater, she tucked her pant legs into her boots. Thank goodness it wasn't raining.

She parked Milligan in the multistory circular parking garage, then hurried down to baggage claim, her heels clicking against the tiled surface.

Cooper was already waiting when she arrived. He didn't notice her, and for a moment she enjoyed just watching him. He looked fresh and vital. It hardly seemed like more than two weeks since she'd last seen him, and yet they'd been the longest weeks of her life.

The morning sunlight filtered unrestrained through the large plate glass windows, glinting on his dark hair. He was tall and broad shouldered. Seeing him again allowed all her pent up feelings to spill over. It took more restraint than she cared to admit not to run into his arms. Instead she adjusted her purse strap over her shoulder, stuffed her hands in her pockets and approached him with a dignified air.

"Good morning, Cooper." She gave him a bright smile, although the muscles at the corners of her mouth trembled with the effort. "It's a beautiful day, isn't it?"

If he was surprised to see her, he hid the shock well. "Ashley," he said, and stood. "Did you bring Madigan with you?" Concern laced his voice.

"Milligan," she corrected and laughed. "You never give up, do you?"

"Not if I can help it." He seemed to struggle with himself for a moment. "How have you been?"

"Sick," she lied unmercifully. "I was in the hospital for several days, doctors said I could have died. But I'm fine now. How about you?" she asked with a flippant air.

"Don't taunt me, Ashley," he warned thickly.

She was deliberately provoking him, but she didn't care. "For all you know it could be true. It's been more than two weeks since

67

I've heard from you."

Turning his gaze to the window, he stood stiffly, watching the sky. "It seems longer," he murmured so low she had to strain to hear.

"Why?" she challenged, standing directly beside him, her own gaze cast toward the heavens.

"How's Webber?" He answered her question with one of his own.

"Webber?" she repeated, her face twisted into a puzzled frown. "You mean Webb?"

"Whoever." He shrugged.

"How do you know about Webb? Oh, wait. Mom." She answered her own question before he had the chance. "Webb and I are friends, nothing more." So this was the way her mother had handled the situation. For a moment fiery resentment burned in her eyes. She loved her mother, but there were times when Sarah Robbins's actions incensed her.

"Your mother mentioned that you and he see a lot of one another." His words were spoken without emotion, as if the subject bored him.

"Friends often do," she returned defensively. "But then, I doubt you'd know that."

She could feel the anger exude from him as he bristled.

"I'm sorry," she whispered, her tone contrite. "I didn't mean that the way it sounded." When she turned her head to look at him, she saw the cold fury leave his eyes. She placed her hand gently on his forearm, drawing his attention to her. "I don't want to argue. Seth and Claudia will know something's wrong, we won't be able to hide it."

He placed his hand on top of hers and squeezed it momentarily. "I don't want to argue, either," he finished. "According to the notice board, their flight has landed."

Ashley's heart fluttered with excitement. "Cooper," she mouthed softly. "My school is having a Christmas party next weekend. Would you . . ." Her tongue stumbled over the words. "I mean, could you . . . would you consider going with me?"

His shocked look cut through her hopes. "Next weekend?"

"The nineteenth . . . it's a Friday night. A dinner party, I don't think it'll be all that formal, just a faculty get together. It's the last day of school, and the dinner is a small celebration."

"Will you be wearing your red cowboy boots?"

"No, I was going to borrow Dad's fishing rubbers," she shot back, then immediately relented. "All right, for you, I'll wear a dress, pantyhose, the whole bit."

Unbuttoning his coat, Cooper took out his cell phone from inside his suit pocket. He punched a few buttons. A frown brought thick brows together. "It seems I've already got plans that night."

Disappointment settled over Ashley. Somehow she'd known he wouldn't accept, that he would find an excuse not to attend.

"I understand," she murmured, but her voice wobbled dangerously.

The silence between them lasted until she saw Claudia, Seth and the boys descending the escalator. As soon as they reached the bottom John broke loose from his father's hand and ran into Cooper's waiting arms.

"Uncle Coop, Uncle Coop!" he cried with childish delight and looped his arms around Cooper's neck. John didn't seem to remember Ashley at first until she offered him a bright smile. "Auntie Ash?" he questioned, holding out his arms to her.

She held out her own arms, and Cooper handed the boy to her. Immediately John spread moist kisses over her cheek. When she glanced over she noticed that Seth and Cooper were enthusiastically shaking hands.

"Ashley," Claudia chimed happily. "I didn't know whether you'd make it to the airport or not. I love your hair."

"So does Webb," she laughed, and had the satisfaction of seeing Cooper's eyes narrow angrily. "And this little angel must be Scott." With John's legs wrapped around her waist, Ashley leaned over to examine the eight-month-old baby in Claudia's arms. "And I bet John's a wonderful big brother, aren't you, John?"

The boy's head bobbed up and down. Both of the Lessinger boys had Seth's dark looks, but their eyes were as blue as a cloudless sky. Claudia's eyes.

Ashley didn't get a chance to talk to her friend until later that afternoon. Both boys were down for a nap, Seth and Cooper were concentrating on a game of chess in Cooper's den, while Ashley and Claudia sat enjoying the view from a bay window in the formal dining room.

"I can't get over how good you look," Claudia said, blowing into a steaming coffee mug. "Your hair really is great."

"The easiest style I've ever had." Ashley ran her fingers through the bouncing curls and shook her head, and her blond locks fell naturally into place.

"Do you see much of Cooper?" Claudia delivered the question with deceptive casualness.

71

"Hardly at all," Ashley replied truthfully. "Why do you ask?"

"I don't know. You two were giving one another odd looks at the airport. I could tell he wasn't pleased with your riding that moped. I thought maybe something was going on between the two of you."

Ashley dismissed Claudia's words with a short shake of her hand. "I'm sure you're mistaken. Can you imagine Cooper Masters being interested in anyone like me?"

"In some ways I can," Claudia insisted. "You two balance one another. He takes everything so seriously, while you finagle your way in and out of anything. I know one thing," she said. "He thinks very highly of you. He has for years."

"You're kidding!"

"I'm not. I don't know that he would have been as happy about me marrying Seth if it hadn't been for you."

"Nonsense," Ashley countered quickly. "I knew you and Seth were right for one another from the first moment I saw you with him. I don't know of any couple who belong together more than you two. And it shows, Claudia, it shows. Your face is radiant. That kind of inner happiness only comes with the deep love of a man."

Claudia's face flushed with color. "I know

it sounds crazy, but I'm more in love with Seth now than when I married him four years ago. I never thought that would be possible. I don't understand how I could have doubted our love and that God wanted us together. My priorities are so different now."

"What about your degree? Do you think you'll ever go back to school?"

"I don't know. Maybe someday, but my life is so full now with the boys I can't imagine squeezing another thing in. I wouldn't want to. John and Scott need me. I suppose when they're older and in school full time I might think about finishing my doctorate, but that's years down the road. I do know that Seth will do whatever he can to help me if I decide to go ahead and get my degree." Pausing, she took another drink from her mug. "What about you? Any man in your life?"

"Several," Ashley teased, without looking at her friend. "None I'm serious about, though."

"What about Webb? You've written about him."

Before Ashley could assure Claudia her relationship with Webb didn't extend beyond a convenient friendship, a dark shadow fell into the room, diverting their attention to the two men who had just entered.

Seth's smile rested on his wife as he crossed the room and placed a loving arm across her shoulders. Cooper remained framed in the archway.

"As usual, Cooper beat the socks off me. I don't know why I bother to play. I can't recall ever beating him."

"What about you, Claudia?" Cooper asked. "You used to play a mean, if a bit unorthodox, game of chess."

Standing, Claudia looped her arm around her husband's waist. "Not me, I'm too tired to concentrate. If everyone will excuse me, I think I'll join the boys and take a nap."

Clenching her mug with both hands, Ashley stood. "I'd better rev up Milligan and get home before the weather —"

"No," Claudia interrupted. "You play Cooper, Ash. You always were a better chess player than me."

Ashley threw a speculative glance toward Cooper, awaiting his reaction. He arched his thick brows in challenge. "Would you care for a game, Miss Robbins?" he asked formally.

Wickedly fluttering her eyelashes, she placed both hands over her heart. "Just what are you suggesting, Mr. Masters?"

Claudia giggled. "You know, suddenly I'm

not the least bit tired."

"Yes, you are," Seth murmured, tightening his grip on his wife's waist. "You and I are going to rest and leave these two to a game of chess."

Claudia didn't object when Seth led her from the room.

"Shall we?" Cooper asked, long strides carrying him to her side. He extended his elbow, and when Ashley placed her arm in his, he gave her a curt nod.

The thought of playing chess with Cooper was an opportunity too good to miss. She was an excellent player and had been the assistant coach for the school's team the year before.

The two leather chairs were pushed opposite one another with a mahogany table standing between. An inlaid board with ivory figures sat atop the table.

"I would like to suggest a friendly wager." The words were offered as a clear challenge.

"Just what are you suggesting?" she asked.

"I'm saying that if I win the match, then you'll accept the new car."

"Honestly, Cooper, you don't give up, do you?"

"Accept the car without any obligation to reimburse me," he continued undaunted, "plus the promise that you'll faithfully drive it to and from work daily."

"And just what do I get if *I* win?" she countered.

"That's up to you."

She released a weary sigh. "I don't think you can give me what I want," she mumbled, lowering her gaze to her hands, laced tightly together in her lap.

"I think I can."

"All right," she added, straightening slightly. "If I win, you must promise never to speak derogatorily of Milligan again, or in any way insinuate that riding my moped is unsafe." He opened and closed his mouth in mute protest. "And in addition I would ask that a generous donation be made to the school's scholarship fund. Agreed?" She could tell he wasn't pleased.

"Agreed." The teasing light left his eyes as he viewed the chess board with a serious look. Taking both a black and a white pawn, he placed them behind his back, then extended his clenched fists for her to choose.

She mumbled a silent prayer, knowing she would have the advantage if she were lucky enough to pick white. Lightly, she tapped his right hand.

Cooper relaxed his fist and revealed the white pawn.

Her spirits soared. He would now be on the defensive.

Neither spoke as they positioned the pieces on the board. A strained, tense air filled the den, and the only sound was the occasional crackle from the fireplace.

Her first move was a standard opening, pawn to king four, which he countered with an identical play. She immediately responded with a gambit, pawn to king's bishop four.

It didn't take her long to impress him with her ability. A smug smile lightly brushed her mouth as she viewed his shock as she gained momentum and dominated the game.

Bending forward, he rubbed a hand across his forehead and then his eyes. Ashley was forced to restrain another smile when he glanced up at her.

"Claudia was right, you *are* a good player."

"Thank you," she responded, hoping to hide the pleasure his acknowledgement gave her.

He made his next move, and she paused to study the board.

"Claudia was right about something else, too," he said softly.

"What's that?" she asked absently, pinching her bottom lip between her thumb and index finger, her concentration centered on the chess board.

"I don't think I've ever told you what an attractive woman you are."

His husky tone seemed to reach out and wrap itself around her. "What'd you say?" Her concentration faltered, and she lifted her gaze to his.

His eyes were narrowed on her mouth. "I said you're beautiful."

The current of awareness between them was so strong that she would gladly have surrendered the game right then and there. She felt close to Cooper, closer than she had to any other person. They had so little in common, and yet they shared the most basic, the strongest, emotion of all. If he had moved or in any way indicated that he wanted her, she would have tossed the chess game aside and wrapped herself in his arms. As it was, her will to win, the determination to prove herself, was quickly lost in the power of his gaze.

"It's your move."

Her eyes darkened with anger as she seethed inwardly. He was playing another game with her, a psychological game in which he had proved to be the clear winner with the first move. Using the attraction she felt for him, he'd hope to derail her concentration. His game read Cooper one, Ashley zilch.

She jumped to her feet and jogged around the room. Pausing to take a series of deep breaths, she took in his cynical look with amusement.

"I hate to appear ignorant here, but just what are you doing?"

"What does it look like?" she countered sarcastically.

"Either you're training for the Olympics or you're sorely testing my limited patience."

"Guess again," she returned impudently, beginning a series of jumping jacks.

"I thought we were playing chess, not twenty questions."

Hands resting challengingly on her hips, she paused and tossed him a brazen glare. "It was either vent my anger physically or punch you out, Cooper Masters."

"Punch me out?" he echoed in disbelief. "What did I do?"

"You know, so don't try to deny it." The anger had dissipated from her blue eyes as she returned to her chair and resumed her study of the board. As the blood pounded in her ears, she knew she'd made a mistake the minute she lifted her hand from the pawn. But would Cooper recognize her error and gain the advantage?

"Cooper?" she whispered.

"Hmm," he answered absently.

"Do you remember the last time I was here?"

He lifted his gaze to hers. "I'm not likely to forget it. After the cold I caught, I coughed for a week."

"Sometimes doing something crazy and irrational has a price." She leaned forward, her chin supported by the palm of her hand.

"Not this time, Ashley Robbins," he gloated, making the one move that would cost her the game. "Check."

CHAPTER 4

Ashley stared at the chess board with a sense of unreality. There was only one move she could make, and she knew what would happen when she took it.

"Checkmate."

She stared at him for a long moment, unable to speak or move. Cooper stood and crossed the room to a huge oak desk that dominated one corner. She watched as he opened a drawer and took out some papers. When he returned to her side, he gave her the car keys.

Her hand was shaking so badly she nearly dropped them.

"This is the registration," he told her, handing her a piece of paper. "After what happened not so long ago, I suggest you keep it in the glove compartment."

Unable to respond with anything more than a nod, she avoided his eyes, which were sure to be sparkling with triumph.

"These are the insurance forms, made out in your name. I believe there's a space for you to sign at the bottom of the policy." He pointed to the large "X" marking the spot, then handed her a pen.

Mutely Ashley complied, but her signature was barely recognizable. She returned the pen.

"I believe that's everything."

"No," she protested, unable to recognize the thin, high voice as her own. "I insist upon paying for the car."

"That wasn't part of our agreement."

"Nonetheless, I insist." She had to struggle to speak clearly.

"No, Ashley," he insisted, "the car is yours."

"But I can't accept something so valuable, not over a silly chess game." She raised her eyes to meet his. Their gazes held, his proud and determined, hers wary and unsure. A muscle moved convulsively at the side of his jaw, and she realized she had lost.

"The car is a gift from me to you. There isn't any way on this earth that I'll accept payment. You were aware of the terms before you agreed to the game."

A painful lump filled her throat, and when she spoke her voice was hoarse. "You have so much," she murmured, her voice cracking. "Must you take my pride, too?" Tears shimmered in the clear depths of her eyes. Wordlessly she left the den, took her coat and walked out the front door. Without a backward glance she climbed aboard Milligan and rode home.

Her mood hadn't improved the next morning as she dressed for church. The sky was dark and threatening, mirroring her temper. How could she love someone as headstrong and narrow minded as Cooper Masters? No wonder his business had grown and prospered over the years. He was ruthless, determined and obstinate.

After tucking her Bible into her backpack, she stepped outside to lock her apartment door. A patch of red in the parking lot caught her attention and she noted that a shiny new car was parked beside Milligan in front of her apartment. As she seethed inwardly, it took great restraint not to vent her anger by kicking the gleaming new car.

The first drops of rain fell lazily to the ground. Even God seemed to be on Cooper's side, she thought, as she heaved a troubled sigh. Either she had to change into her rain gear or drive the car. She chose the latter. Pulling out of the parking lot, she was forced to admit the car handled like a dream. Ashley was prepared to hate the car, but it didn't even take the full five miles to church for her to acknowledge she was going to love this car. Just as much as she loved the man who had given it to her.

As the Sunday School teacher for the three-year-olds, she was excited that John Lessinger would be in her class.

Claudia dropped him off at the classroom, Scotty resting on her hip, the diaper bag dangling from her arm.

"Morning." Ashley beamed warmly. "How's Johnny?" She directed her attention to the small boy who hid behind Claudia's skirts.

"He's playing shy today," Claudia warned.

"I don't blame him," Ashley whispered in return. "A lot's happened in the last couple of days."

"I'll drop Scotty off at the nursery and come back to see how John does."

"He'll be fine," Ashley assured her. "Did you see the playdough, Johnny?" she asked, directing his attention to the low table where several other children were busy playing. "Come over here and I'll introduce you to some of my friends."

John's look was unsure, and he glanced over his shoulder at his retreating mother. His lower lip began to quiver as tears welled in his blue eyes. Kneeling down to his level, Ashley placed her hands on his small shoulders. "Johnny, it's Auntie Ash. You remember me, don't you? There's nothing to frighten you here. Come over and meet Joseph and Matthew. You can tell them all about Alaska."

John was playing nicely with the other children when Claudia returned. She sighed in relief. "Now I can relax," she whispered. "I don't know what it is about men and Sunday mornings, but it takes Seth twice as long as me to get ready. Then I'm left to carry Scott, steer John, haul the diaper bag, the Bibles and my purse, while Seth can't manage anything more than his car keys."

Ashley stifled a giggle. She allowed the children to play for several more minutes, chatting with Claudia, who insisted on staying for the first part of Sunday school to be sure John was really all right.

Ashley gathered the children in a circle and had them sit on the patch of carpet in the middle of the floor. As she sat cross-legged on the floor with them, one of the shyer children came over and seated herself in Ashley's lap. "I'm glad we're all together, together, together," the little girl sang in a sweet, melodious voice. "Because Jesus is here, and teacher's here, and —"

"Cooper's here," Claudia chimed in softly.

The song died on the girl's lips as everyone looked over at the tall, compelling figure standing in the open door. His attention was centered on Ashley and the little girl in her lap. For a moment he seemed to go pale, and the muscles in his jaw jerked, and Ashley wondered what she had done now to anger him. Without a word, he pivoted and left the room.

"I'd better see what he wanted," Claudia said, following him out of the room.

Ashley didn't see either of them again until it was time for the morning worship service. The four adults sat together, Claudia between her and Cooper. A hundred questions whirled in her mind. How had Claudia gotten Cooper to attend church? It wasn't all that long ago that he had scoffed at her friend's newfound faith. She wondered if Seth had some influence on Cooper's decision to attend church. More than likely John had said something, and Cooper had been unable to refuse.

Just as the pastor stepped in front of the congregation to light the third candle of the Advent wreath, a loud cry came from the nursery.

Claudia emitted a low groan. "Scotty." She leaned over and whispered to Ashley, "I wasn't sure I'd be able to leave him this long." She stood and made her way out of the pew. Cooper closed the space separating them.

Never had Ashley been more aware of a man's presence. As his thigh lightly touched hers, she closed her eyes at the potency of the contact. Nervously she scooted away, putting some space between them. When he turned and looked at her an unfamiliar quality had entered his eyes. He smiled, one of those rare smiles that came from his heart and nearly stopped hers. Its overwhelming force left her exposed and completely vulnerable. Undoubtedly he would be able to read the effect he had on her and know her thoughts. Quickly turning her face away, she squeezed her eyes closed, and then the pastor, the service, everything, everyone, was lost as Cooper closed his hand firmly over hers.

In all the years she had loved Cooper, Ashley had never dared to dream that he would sit beside her in church or share her strong faith. The intense sensations of having him near touched her so dramatically that for a moment she was sure her heart would burst with unrestrained happiness.

His grip remained tight and firm until Claudia returned to the pew and sat beside

Seth. Immediately Cooper released Ashley's hand. The happiness that had filled her so briefly was gone. He seemed content to hold her hand only as long as no one knew. The minute someone came, he let her go.

Once again she was forcefully reminded of the huge differences that separated them. He was a corporate manager, a powerful, wealthy man. She was a financially struggling schoolteacher. In some ways she was certain he cared for her, but not enough to admit it openly. She sometimes feared she was an embarrassment to him, a fear that had dogged her from the beginning.

"Did you win the Irish Sweepstakes?" Webb asked Ashley as she pulled into the school parking lot and climbed out of the shining new car.

"No," she said and sighed unhappily. "I lost a chess game."

He gave her a funny look. "Let me make certain I've got this straight. You *lost* the chess game and won the car?"

"You got it."

Rubbing the side of his chin with one hand, he stared at her with confused eyes. "I know there's logic in this someplace, but for the moment it's escaped me."

"I wouldn't doubt it," she said, and nodded a friendly greeting to the school secretary as she walked through the door.

"What would you have gotten if you'd *won?*" Webb asked as he followed on her heels.

"Milligan and my pride."

"That's another one of those answers that seems to have gone right over my head." He waved his hand over the top of his blond head in illustration. Confusion clouded his eyes. "All I really want to know is whether this person likes chess and plays often? It wouldn't be hard for me to lose. I don't even like the game."

"You wouldn't want to play this person," she mumbled under her breath, heading toward the faculty room.

"Don't be hasty, Ashley," he countered quickly. "Let me be the judge of that."

Tossing him a look she usually reserved for rowdy students was enough to quell his curiosity.

"We're going to the Christmas party Friday night, aren't we?" he asked, steering clear of the former topic of discussion.

Releasing a slow breath, Ashley cupped a coffee mug with both hands. Her enthusiasm for the party had disappeared with Cooper's excuse not to attend. Probably because she believed that the previous appointment he claimed to have was merely a pretext to avoid refusing her outright.

"I don't know, I have a friend visiting from Alaska," she said before sipping. "We may be doing something that night."

"Sure, no problem," he said with a smile. "Let me know if you change your mind."

No pleading, no hesitation, no regrets. The least he could do was show some remorse over her missing the party. As she watched him saunter out of the faculty room, she threw imaginary daggers at his back. Unhappy and more than a little depressed, she finished her coffee and went to her homeroom.

"Is there something drastically wrong with me?" Ashley asked Claudia later that afternoon. She'd stopped by after school for a short visit with Claudia and the boys before Cooper returned from his office.

When Claudia looked up from bouncing Scotty on her knee, her eyes showed surprise. "Heavens, no. What makes you ask?"

"I mean, you'd tell me if I had bad breath or something, wouldn't you?"

"You know me well enough to answer that."

As Johnny weaved a toy truck around the chair legs, then pushed it under the table to the far side of the room, Ashley's eyes followed the movement of her godson. Lowering her face, she took a deep breath, afraid she might do something stupid like cry. "I want to get married and have children. I'm twenty-six and not getting any younger."

"I'm sure there are plenty of men out there who'd be interested. Only yesterday Seth was saying how pretty you've gotten. Surely there's someone —"

"That's just it," Ashley interrupted, knowing she couldn't mention Cooper. "There isn't, and I found a gray hair the other day. I'm getting scared."

"You and Cooper both. Have you noticed how he's getting gray along his sideburns? It really makes him look distinguished, doesn't it?"

Ashley agreed with a smile, but her eyes refused to meet her friend's, afraid she wouldn't be able to disguise her feelings for Cooper.

"Oh, before I forget, Seth and I have been invited to a dinner party this Friday night, and we were wondering if you could watch the boys. If you have plans just say so, because I think your mother might be able to do it."

Some devilish impulse made her ask, "What about Cooper?"

"He's got some appointment he can't get out of."

For a startled second the oxygen seemed trapped in Ashley's lungs. He had been telling the truth. He *did* have an appointment. In that brief second the sun took on a brighter intensity; it was as if the birds began to chirp.

"I'd love to stay with John and Scott," she returned enthusiastically. "We'll have a wonderful time, won't we, boys?" Neither one looked especially pleased. Glancing at her watch, Ashley quickly stood. "I've gotta scoot, I'll see you Friday. What time do you want me?"

"Is six too early? I'll try to get the boys fed and dressed."

"Don't do that," Ashley admonished with a laugh. "It'll be good practice for me. I need to learn all this motherhood stuff, you know."

"Don't rush off," Claudia said. "Cooper will be home any minute."

"I can't stay. Tell him I said hello — no, don't," she added abruptly. He might have been telling the truth about being busy Friday night, but it didn't lessen the hurt of his rejection. "Mid-year reports go home this Friday, and I want to get a head start."

Claudia regarded her quizzically as she

walked her to the door. "Thanks again for Friday. I don't like to leave the boys with strangers. It's bad enough for them to be away from home."

"Happy to help," Ashley said sincerely. Giving a tiny wave to both boys, she smiled when Scotty raised his chubby hand to her. Johnny ran to the front window to look out, and Ashley played peek-a-boo with him. The small head had just bobbed out from behind the drapes when Cooper spoke from behind her.

"Hello, Ashley."

She stiffened at the sound of his voice, her heartbeat racing double time. Last Sunday at church had been the last time she'd seen him.

"Hello." Her voice was devoid of any warmth or welcome. He looked dignified in his suit and silk tie. Childishly she was upset at him all the more for it.

"Is something the matter?" he asked in a quiet voice.

"No," she answered, her gaze stern and unyielding. "I'm just surprised that you'd taint your image by being seen with me."

"What are you talking about?"

"If you don't know, then I'm not going to tell you."

His gaze narrowed. "What's wrong? Obviously something's troubling you."

"The man's a genius," she replied flippantly. "Now, if you'll excuse me, I'll be on my way."

Cooper's eyes contained a hard gleam she had never seen. His hand shot out and gripped her upper arm. "Tell me what's going on in that unpredictable mind of yours."

Defiance flared from her as she stared pointedly at his hand until he relaxed his hold. Breaking free, she took a few steps in retreat, creating the breathing space she needed to vent her frustration. "I'll have you know, Cooper Masters, I'm not the least bit ashamed of who or what I am. My mother may be your housekeeper, but she has served you well all these years. My father's a skilled sheet metal worker, and I'm proud of them both. I don't have a thing to be ashamed about. Not in front of you or anyone." Having finished her tirade, she avoided looking at him and walked straight to her car.

She never made it. A strong hand on her shoulder swung her around, pinning her against the side of the car. "What are you implying?" The tone of his voice made Ashley shudder. His nostrils flared with barely restrained fury.

Tears shimmered in her eyes until his face

was swimming before her. She bit her bottom lip. Suddenly she could feel the anger drain out of him.

"What's the matter with us?" he demanded hoarsely, then expelled an impatient breath.

"Everything!" she cried, her voice trembling. "Everything," she repeated. When she struggled, he released her and didn't try to stop her again. He stepped back as she climbed inside the car, revved the engine, and drove away.

If Ashley was miserable then, it was nothing compared to the way she felt later. To soothe away her emotional turmoil and frustration, she filled the bathtub with hot water and bubble bath, and soaked in it until the water became tepid. In an attempt to pray, she tried the conversational approach that had come so naturally to her in the past, but even that was impossible in her present state of mind.

Sleep was a long time coming that night. She couldn't seem to find a comfortable position, and when she did drift off she found herself trapped in a dream of hopelessness. Waking early the next morning, she rose before the alarm sounded, put on the coffee and sat in the dark, shadow-filled room waiting for the first light.

Lackadaisically, she reached for her devotional and discovered the suggested reading for the day was the famous love chapter in First Corinthians, Chapter Thirteen. *Love is very patient and kind,* verse four stated.

Had she been patient? Ten years seemed a long time to her, and that was how long it had been since she first realized she'd loved Cooper. Since the tender age of sixteen. Glancing back to her Bible, she continued reading. *Love doesn't demand its own way. It isn't irritable or touchy. It doesn't hold grudges and will hardly notice when others do wrong. . . . If you love someone you will always believe in him, always expect the best of him, and always stand your ground in defending him.*

Closing her Bible, Ashley released an uneven breath. It looked as though she had a long way to go to achieve the standards God had set.

When it came time for her to pray, she got down on her knees, meditating first on the words she had read. Ever since Sunday she'd expected the worst from Cooper, thought the worst of him. She'd wanted to explain how hurt she was, but it sounded so petty to accuse him of being ashamed of her because he'd quit holding her hand. In voicing her thoughts, the whole incident sounded ludicrous. It seemed she was building things in her own mind because she was insecure. The same thoughts had come to her the night he'd taken her to the Italian restaurant, and the night Claudia had phoned from Alaska. She'd never thought of herself as someone with low self-esteem before Cooper.

"Oh, ye of little faith," she said aloud. *No,* her heart countered, *ye of little love.*

Ashley hummed cheerfully as she pulled into the school parking lot. She was proud of the fact that she had worked things out in her own mind — with God's help, of course. The next time she saw Cooper, she would apologize for her behavior and ask that they start again. Poor man, he wouldn't know what to think. One minute she was ranting and raving, and the next she was apologizing.

Today was a special day for her Senior Literature class. They'd been reading and studying the Western classic *The Oxbow Incident* by Walter Van Tilburg Clark. As part of her preparation for their final exam, Ashley dressed up as one of the characters in the book. Portraying the part as believably as possible, she was usually able to draw out heated discussions and points that might otherwise have been glossed over.

Today she was dressing as Donald Martin, one of the three men accused of cattle rustling in the powerful narrative. This was always Ashley's favorite part of the quarter, and her classroom antics were well known.

Her afternoon students were buzzing with speculation when the bell rang. She waited until everyone was seated before she came through the door to be greeted by laughter and cheers. She was wearing a ten gallon hat. Her cowboy boots had silver spurs, and her long, slim legs were disguised by leather chaps. Two toy six-shooters were holstered at her hips. With her hair tucked under the hat, she'd made a token attempt toward realism by smearing dirt over her creamy smooth cheeks and pasting a long black mustache across her upper lip.

The class loved it, and immediate speculation arose about what character she was portraying.

"I'm here today to talk about mob justice," she began, sitting on the corner of her desk and dangling one foot over the edge.

"She's Gil," one of the boys in the back row called out.

"Good guess, David," she said, pointing to him. "But I'm no drifter. I own my own spread at Pike's Hole. Me and the Missus are building up our herd."

"It's Mex," someone else shouted.

"No way," Diana Crosby corrected. "Mex wasn't married."

"Good girl, Diana." She twirled both six-shooters around a couple of times and by pure luck happened to place them in the holsters right side up. When her class applauded she bowed, her hat falling off her head. As she bent to pick it up she noticed a face staring at her from the small glass portion of the class door. The face was lovingly familiar. Cooper.

"If you'll excuse me a minute, I have to check my horse," she said, quickly making up a pretense to escape into the hallway.

"What are you doing here?" she demanded in a low tone.

A smile danced in his eyes as he attempted to hide his grin by rubbing his thumb across the angular line of his jaw. "Butch Cassidy, I presume."

"Cooper, I'm in the middle of class," she muttered with an exaggerated sigh, both hands gripping his arms. "But I'm so glad to see you. I feel terrible about the way I acted yesterday. I was wrong, terribly wrong."

The laughter faded from his features as he

regarded her seriously. "I had no idea the dinner party meant so much to you."

"What dinner party?" He was talking in riddles.

"The one you asked me to attend with you. I assumed that was what upset you yesterday."

She shook her head in wry dismay. "No . . . that wasn't it."

"Then what was?"

Casting an apprehensive glare over her shoulder, she turned pleading eyes to him. "I can't talk now."

He rubbed a weary hand over his face. "Ashley, I rearranged my schedule. I'll be happy to take you to the school Christmas party."

She groaned softly. "But I can't go now."

"What do you mean, you can't go?" His dark, steely eyes narrowed.

He didn't need to say another word for her to know how much it had inconvenienced him to readjust his schedule.

"Cooper, I'm sorry, but I . . ."

"Invited someone else," he finished for her, his eyes as cold as a blast of arctic wind. "That Webber fellow, I imagine."

"I haven't got time to stand in the hall and argue with you. My class is waiting."

"And so, I imagine, is Webber."

Fury blazed in her eyes as she slashed him a cutting look. "You do that on purpose."

"Do what?" His voice was barely civil.

"Call Webb 'Webber,' the same way you call Milligan 'Madigan.' I find the whole denial thing rather childish," she snapped resentfully. By now she was too incensed to care if she was making sense.

"I find that statement unworthy of comment."

"You would." She spun away and stalked back into the classroom, restraining the impulse to slam the door.

Claudia was dressed in a mauve-colored chiffon evening gown that was a stunning complement to her auburn hair and cream coloring. Seth, too, looked remarkably attractive in his suit and tie.

"Okay, I showed you where everything is in the bedroom, and here's the phone number of the restaurant." Claudia laid the pad near the phone in the kitchen. "I've left a baby bottle in the refrigerator, but I've already nursed Scotty, so he probably won't need it."

"Okay," Ashley said, following Claudia out of the kitchen.

"Both boys are dressed for bed, and don't let either of them stay up past eight-thirty.

You may need to rock Scotty to sleep."

"No problem, I got my degree in rocking chair."

Checking her reflection in the hallway mirror, Claudia tucked a stray hair back into her coiled French coiffure. "You didn't happen to have an argument with Cooper, did you?" The question came out of the blue.

Ashley could feel the blood rush from her face, then just as quickly flood back. "What makes you ask?"

"Seth and I have hardly seen him the last couple of days, and he's been in the foulest mood. It's not like him to behave like this. I can't understand it."

"What makes you think I have anything to do with it?" she asked, doing her best to conceal her reaction.

"I know it sounds crazy, and I wouldn't want to offend you, Ash, but I still think something's stirring between you two. I may be an old married fuddy-duddy, but I recognize the looks he's been giving you. What I can't understand is why the two of you work so hard at hiding it. As far as I'm concerned, you're perfect for one another."

"Ha," Ashley said harshly. "We can't spend two minutes together lately without going for each other's jugular."

Seth took Claudia's wrap from the hall

closet and placed it over her shoulders. "Sounds like the way it was with us a few times, doesn't it, Honey?" he asked, and tenderly kissed the creamy smooth slope of Claudia's neck.

"Call if you have any problems, won't you?" Claudia said, suddenly sounding worried. "Scotty will cry the first few minutes after we've left, but he should quiet down in a little bit, so don't panic."

"I never panic," Ashley assured her with a cheeky grin.

True to his mother's word, Scott gave a hearty cry the minute the door was closed.

"It's all right. Look, here's your teddy."

Scotty took the stuffed animal, threw it across the room and cried all the louder.

Ten minutes passed and nothing seemed to calm his frantic cries. Even John looked as if he was ready to give way and start howling.

"Come on, sweetie, not you, too."

"I want my mommy."

"Let's pretend I'm your mommy," Ashley offered, "and then you can tell me how to make Scotty happy."

"Will you hold me like my mommy?" Johnny asked, a tear running down his pale face.

"Sure, join the crowd," Ashley laughed,

lifting him so that she had a baby on each hip. Johnny cried in small whimpering sounds and Scott in large howling sobs.

Pacing the floor, she glanced up to find Cooper standing in the entryway watching her, a stunned look on his face.

CHAPTER 5

"Look, Johnny, Scott," Ashley said cheerfully. "Uncle Cooper's here."

Both boys cried harder. Scotty buried his
face in her neck, his stubby hands tangled
in her blond hair. When he pulled a long
strand, she cried out involuntarily, "Ouch."

The small protest spurred Cooper into action. He hung his overcoat in the hall closet
and entered the living room, taking John
from Ashley.

"What's the matter, fella?" he asked in a
reassuring tone.

"I want my mommy!" John wailed.

"They went out for the evening," Ashley
explained, both hands supporting Scott as
she paced the floor, making cooing sounds
in his ear. But nothing seemed to comfort
the baby, who continued to cry pitifully.

"What about Webber and your party?"
Cooper asked stiffly.

"I tried to tell you that I wasn't going,"

she explained, and breathed in deeply. "I didn't say a thing about attending the party with Webb. You assumed I was."

"Are you telling me the reason you didn't go tonight is because you'd promised to baby-sit John and Scotty?"

Ashley silently confirmed the statement with a weak nod. His dark eyes narrowed with self-directed anger.

"Why do you put up with me?" he asked.

She didn't get the opportunity to answer, because Scotty began bellowing even louder.

A troubled frown broke across Cooper's expression. "Is he sick? I've never heard him cry like that."

"No, just unhappy. Claudia said she'd left a bottle for him. Maybe we should heat it up."

All four moved into the kitchen. With Scotty balanced on her hip, Ashley took the baby bottle out of the refrigerator. "It needs to be heated." She held it out to him.

"If you say so," he said, shrugging his broad shoulders. "How does your mommy do it?" he asked Johnny, who seemed more secure now that his uncle had arrived.

"She nurses Scotty."

Slowly Cooper's dark eyes met hers, amusement flickering across his face. She giggled, and soon they were both laughing.

Scotty cried all the harder, clinging to Ashley.

The humor broke the terrible tension that had existed between them for days.

Cooper smiled warmly into her eyes, trying to hold back his laughter. He walked across the room and took a large pan out of the bottom cupboard, then filled it with hot water. "I don't want to chance the microwave. What if I melt the bottle? It's plastic, after all." By the time he'd set the pan on the stove and turned on the burner, he'd regained his composure.

Ashley placed the baby bottle in the water. "Is it supposed to float?"

"I don't know." He shook his head briefly, the look in his eyes unbelievably tender.

"Oh well, we'll experiment, won't we, boys?"

"What's an experiment?" Johnny asked. He was sitting on top of the counter, his short legs dangling over the edge.

"It's a process by which we examine the validity of a hypothesis and determine the nature of something as yet unknown."

"Cooper . . ." Ashley laughed at the way the three-year-old's mouth and eyes rounded as he tried to understand what Cooper was saying. "Honestly! Let me explain." She turned to Johnny. "An experiment is trying something you've never done before."

"Oh!" Johnny's clouded expression brightened, and he eagerly shook his head. "Mommy does that a lot with dinner."

"That's right." Ashley beamed.

"Smart aleck," Cooper whispered under his breath, his gaze lingering on her for a heart-stopping moment.

Ashley found herself drowning in the dark depths of his eyes and quickly averted her head. The water in the pan was coming to a boil, the baby bottle tossing back and forth in the bubbling liquid.

"It must be ready by now," she commented as she turned off the burner.

Cooper went out to the back porch and returned with a huge pair of barbeque tongs. He quickly lifted the bottle from the hot water, setting it upright on the counter.

"Nicely done," she commented, and waited a few minutes before testing the milk's temperature. Once she was sure it wouldn't burn Scotty's tender mouth, she led the way into the living room.

Remembering what Claudia had said about rocking the baby, Ashley sat in the polished wooden rocker and gently tipped back and forth. Scotty reached for the bottle and held it himself, sucking greedily. Her eyes filled with tenderness. She brushed the fine hair from his face and cupped his ear. The room was blissfully silent as John and Cooper sat across from her.

Johnny crawled into Cooper's lap and handed him a book that he wanted read. Cooper complied, his voice and face expressive as he turned page after page, reading quietly.

Ashley found her attention drawn again and again to the man and the young boy. A surge of love filled her, so strong and overpowering that tears formed in her eyes. Hurriedly she looked away, batting her eyelashes to forestall the moisture.

Losing interest in the bottle, Scotty began chewing the nipple and watching Ashley. His round eyes held a fascinated expression as he studied her hair and reached out to grab her blond curls.

Carefully, she brushed her hair back. As she did her eyes met Cooper's. His gaze had centered on her mouth with a disturbing intensity. The power he had over her produced an aching tightness in her throat.

"You'll make a good mother someday." His voice was low and husky.

"I was just thinking the same thing about you," she murmured, then realizing what she'd said and hastened to correct herself.

"I mean a good father."

"I know what you meant."

"Uncle Cooper." Johnny tugged at Cooper's arm. "You're supposed to be reading."

"So I am," he agreed in a lazy drawl. "So I am."

Finished now, Scotty tossed the bottle aside, then struggled to sit up. "I know I should burp him," Ashley said, "but I'm not sure of the best way to hold him."

Cooper stood. "Claudia left a baby book lying around here somewhere. Maybe it would be best to look it up."

The small party moved into Cooper's den. Ashley carried Scotty on her hip. He didn't make a sound, having apparently become accustomed to her, and that pleased her.

Cooper found the book and set it on his desk, flipping the pages. As soon as Ashley bent over next to him to read a paragraph, Scotty burped loudly.

"Well I guess that answers that, doesn't it?" she said, laughing.

"Uncle Coop, can I have a piggy back ride?" Johnny climbed onto the chair and held out his hands entreatingly.

Cooper looked unsure for a moment but agreed with a good-natured nod. "Okay, partner."

Johnny climbed onto Cooper's back,

looped his legs around his uncle's waist and clung tightly with his chubby arms. "Gitty-up, horsey," he commanded happily.

Cooper grinned. "How come this is called a piggyback ride and you say 'Gitty-up, horsey'?"

Johnny chuckled. "It's an experiment."

"He's got you there." Ashley flashed him a cheeky grin.

Cooper mumbled something unintelligible and trotted into the next room.

Ashley followed, enjoying the sight of Cooper looking so relaxed. Scotty clapped his hands gleefully, and Ashley trotted after the others.

After a moment Cooper paused. "I smell something."

"Not . . ." She didn't finish.

"I think it must be."

Three pairs of eyes centered on the baby. Dramatically, Johnny plugged his nose. "Scotty has a messy diaper," he announced with the formality of a judge.

"Well, he's still a baby, and they're expected to do that sort of thing. Isn't that right, Scotty?"

Unconcerned, Scotty cooed happily, chewing on his pajama sleeve.

"Claudia showed me where everything is, this shouldn't take long."

"Ashley." Cooper stopped her, his face tight. "I think I should probably be the one to change him."

"You? Why? Are you saying it's the proper thing to do, since he's a boy?"

"I'm saying it's not a lot of fun and I've done it before, so . . ."

Unsuccessfully disguising a grateful smile, she handed him the baby. Scotty protested loudly as Cooper supported him with his hands under the baby's armpits, holding him as far away as possible.

"Call me if you need help."

Johnny led the way up the stairs, the large wooden steps almost more than he could manage. Cooper glanced down, his brow marred by a frown, then followed his nephew down the hall.

Ashley waited at the foot of the stairs, one shoe positioned on the bottom step, in case Cooper called.

"Auntie Ash." Johnny came running down the wide hallway and stopped at the top of the stairs. "Uncle Cooper says he needs you."

A tiny smile formed lines at the edges of her mouth. Somehow the words sounded exceedingly beautiful. She yearned to hear them from Cooper himself, though not exactly in this context.

She entered the bedroom and saw that his frown had deepened. He extended a hand to stop her as she entered the nursery. "I need a washcloth or something . . . you can give it to John."

Ashley ran the water in the bathroom sink until it was warm and soaked the washcloth in it. After wringing out most of the moisture, she handed it to Johnny, who ran full speed into the bedroom.

Loitering outside the room, Ashley impatiently stuck her head inside the door. "Cooper, this is silly."

"I'm almost finished," he mumbled. "This was just a little . . . more than I'm used to dealing with." His expensive silk tie was loosened, and the long sleeves of his crisp business shirt had been rolled up to his elbows.

Ashley watched from the doorway, highly amused.

"Voilà," he said, pleased with himself, as he stood Scotty up on the table.

Ashley dissolved into fits of laughter. The disposable diaper stuck out at odd angles in every direction. Had he really done this before, or had he just been trying to spare her an unpleasant task? As she was giggling, the diaper began to slide down Scotty's legs, stopping at knee level. She laughed so hard that her shoulders shook.

"Here, let me try," she insisted after a moment, swallowing her amusement as best she could.

Cooper looked almost grateful when she took the baby and laid him back onto the changing table. She did the best she could, but her efforts weren't much better than Cooper's. He was kind enough not to comment.

When she had finished, she paused to look around the room for the first time. Claudia had told her about the bedroom Cooper had decorated for the boys, but she hadn't had a chance to take it all in earlier. Now she could stand back and marvel. The walls were painted blue, with cotton candy clouds floating past and a huge multicolored rainbow with a pot of gold.

Johnny, who had apparently noticed her appreciation, tugged at her hand. "Come look."

Obligingly, Ashley followed.

He closed the door, and flipped the light switch, casting the room into darkness. "See," he said, pointing to the ceiling.

Ashley looked up and noticed a hundred glittering stars illuminated on the huge ceiling. What had been an attractive, whimsical room with the light on became a land of fantasy with the light off.

"It's great," she murmured, her voice slightly thick. Over and over again Claudia had commented on how much Cooper loved the boys. Ashley had seen it herself. He wasn't lofty or untouchable when he was with John and Scott. His affinity for children showed he could be human and vulnerable. He was so warm and loving with the boys that it was all she could do to keep from running into his arms.

Cooper made a show of checking his wristwatch. "Isn't it about time for you boys to go to bed?"

"Can I wear your watch again?" Johnny asked eagerly.

Cooper didn't hesitate, slipping the gold band from his wrist and placing it on his godson's arm.

Ashley couldn't help but wonder at the ease with which Cooper relinquished a timepiece that must have cost thousands of dollars.

Scotty cried when she placed him in the crib. She stayed for several minutes, attempting to comfort him, but to no avail. She would just get him to lie down and tuck him under the blanket when he would pull himself upright, hold onto the bars and look at her with those pleading blue eyes. She couldn't refuse, and finally gave in and lifted him out of the crib.

"Claudia said something about rocking him to sleep."

"No problem," Cooper said with a sly grin. He left and returned a minute later with the wooden rocker from downstairs.

"Will you pray with me, Uncle Cooper?" Johnny — who was also still wide awake — requested, kneeling at his bedside.

Cooper joined the little boy on the plush navy blue carpet.

For the second time that night Ashley was emotionally stirred by the sight of this man with a child.

"God bless Mommy, Daddy and Scotty," John prayed, his head bowed reverently, his small hands folded. "And God bless Uncle Cooper, Auntie Ash and all the angels. And I love you, Jesus, and amen."

"Amen," Cooper echoed softly.

Scotty had his eyes closed as he lay securely in Ashley's arms. Gently she stood to lay him in the crib, but both eyes flew open anxiously and he struggled to sit up. With a short sigh of acquiescence, she sat back down and began to rock again. Content, Scotty watched her, but with every minute his eyes closed a little more. She wouldn't make the mistake of getting up too early a second time. Gently, she brushed the wisps of hair from his brow.

Cooper was sitting on the mattress beside Johnny, who was playing with the wristwatch, his gaze fixed on the lighted digits. Cooper pushed a variety of buttons, which delighted the boy. After a few minutes, Cooper tucked Johnny between the sheets and leaned over to kiss his brow.

"Night, night, Auntie Ash," Johnny whispered.

She blew him a kiss. Johnny pretended to catch it, then tucked his stuffed animal under his arm and rolled over.

The moment was serene and peaceful. Finally sure that Scotty was asleep, she stood and gently put him into the crib. Cooper came to stand at her side, a hand cupping her shoulder as they looked down on the sleeping baby.

Neither spoke, afraid of destroying the tranquility. When they finally stepped back, he removed his hand. Immediately, Ashley missed the warmth of his touch as they headed back downstairs.

He paused at the bottom of the stairs, a step ahead of her. He turned, halting her descent.

"Ashley," he whispered on a soft trembling breath, his look dark and troubled.

A tremor ran through her at the perplexing expression she saw in his eyes. Spontaneously she slipped her arms around his neck without even being aware of what she was doing.

"Ashley," he repeated, the husky sound a gentle caress. He crushed her to him, his arms hugging her waist as his lips sought hers. The kiss was like it had always been between them. That jolt of awareness so strong it seemed to catch them both off guard. When his mouth broke from hers, she could hear his labored breathing and the heavy thud of his heart.

He loosened his hold, bringing his hands up to her neck, weaving long fingers through her hair. His lips soothed her chin and temple, and she gloried in the tingling sensations that spread through her. She continued to lean against him, needing his support, because her legs felt weak and wobbly.

"I'm sorry about the party tonight," he murmured, and she couldn't doubt the sincerity in his voice.

"No, I'm the one who should be sorry. I said so many terrible things to you." Tipping her head back so she could gaze into his impassioned eyes, she spoke again. "I'm amazed you put up with me." Lovingly, she traced the proud line of his jaw, a finger paused to investigate the tiny cleft in his chin. Unable to resist, she kissed him there and loved the sound of his groan.

"Ashley," he warned, "please, it's hard enough keeping my hands off you."

"It is? Really? Oh, Cooper, really?"

"Yes, so don't tease."

"I think that's the nicest thing you've ever said to me."

His hand curved around her waist as he brought her down the last step. "Have you eaten dinner?"

"No, I didn't have time. You?"

"I'm starved. Maybe we can dig up something in the kitchen."

She couldn't see why they needed to look for anything. Her mother did the cooking for him, and there were bound to be leftovers. "Mom —"

"I gave her the rest of the month off," he explained before she could finish.

"Well, in that case, I vote for pizza."

"Pizza?" He glanced at her, aghast.

"All right, you choose." She placed an arm around him and smiled deeply into his dark eyes.

"Let's look." Together they rounded the corner that led to the kitchen. He checked the refrigerator and turned, shaking his head. "I don't know how we'd manage to make pizza from any of this."

"Not make," she corrected. "Order. All we need to do is phone and wait for the delivery guy."

"Amazing." He tilted his head at an inquiring angle. "Is this something you and this Webber fellow do often?"

A denial rose automatically to her lips, but she successfully swallowed it back. "Sometimes. And his name is Dennis Webb."

The corner of his mouth lifted in a half-smile. "Sorry." But he didn't look the least bit repentant.

"Do you want me to order?"

He straightened and leaned against the kitchen counter. "Sure, whatever you want."

"Canadian bacon, pineapple and olives."

His dark eyes widened questioningly, but he nodded his agreement.

She couldn't help laughing. "It tastes great, trust me."

"I'm afraid I'll have to."

She used the phone in the kitchen. Cooper regarded her suspiciously when she punched in the number without looking it up in the directory.

"You know the number by heart? Just how often do you do this?"

"I'm good with numbers."

After placing their order, she turned and smiled seductively. "Shall we play a game of chess while we're waiting?"

His look was faintly mocking. "I have a feeling I'd better not."

"Why?" she asked, batting her long lashes.

"If I say yes, then no wagers," he insisted.

"You take all the fun out of it," she said, and feigned a pout. "But I'll manage to whip you anyway."

He chuckled and took her hand, leading them into his den.

While she set up the game board, Cooper lit the logs in the fireplace. Within minutes flickering shadows played across the walls.

His eyes were serious as he sat down opposite her. As before, each move was measured and thought-filled. At mid-game the advantage was Ashley's. Then the doorbell chimed, interrupting their concentration.

Cooper answered and returned with a huge flat box, his look slightly abashed. "You ordered enough for a family of five," he chastised her.

"You said you were hungry," she argued, not lifting her gaze from the game. Her eyes brightened as she moved and captured his knight, lifting it from the board.

"How'd you do that?" His expression

turned serious as he set the pizza on the hearth to keep warm. "I don't want to stop now. We can eat later."

"I'm hungry," she insisted slyly.

He waved her away with the flick of his hand, his attention centered on the board. "You go ahead and eat, then."

She left the room and returned a minute later with a plate and napkin, sitting on the floor in front of the fire. The aroma of melted cheese and Canadian bacon filled the room when she lifted the lid. "Yumm, this is delicious," she said after swallowing her first bite.

A frown drove three wide creases into his brow as he glanced up. "You're eating in here," he said, as if noticing her for the first time.

"I'm not supposed to?" Color invaded her face until her cheeks felt hot. She was always doing something she shouldn't where Cooper was concerned. Her actions had probably shocked him. No doubt he had never in his entire life eaten any place but on a table with a linen cloth. Pizza on the floor made her look childish and gauche.

His expression softened. "It's fine, I'm sure. It's just that I never have."

"Oh." She felt ridiculously close to tears and bowed her head. The pizza suddenly tasted like glue. She closed the lid, then set her plate aside. "The carpet is probably worth a fortune. I wouldn't want to ruin it," she said with total sincerity.

He put a finger under her chin and raised her eyes to his. "Shh," he whispered, and gently laid his mouth over hers.

His kiss had been unexpected, catching her off guard, but quickly she became a willing victim.

"You're right," Cooper murmured, then chuckled. "The pizza does taste good." He lowered himself onto the floor beside her and helped himself to a piece. "Delicious," he agreed, his eyes smiling.

"Can I have a taste?" she asked, a faint smile curving her mouth.

He held out the triangular wedge. She leaned forward and carefully took a bite.

"Thank you," she told him seriously.

With slow, deliberate movements, he placed the pizza box, plates and napkins aside, and reached for her.

Ashley moved willingly into his arms. Sliding her hands around his neck, she raised her face, eager for his attention. Her mouth was trembling in anticipation when he claimed it. A feeling of warmth wove its way through her and seemed to touch Cooper as the kiss deepened.

Somewhere, a long way in the distance, a bell began to chime. Fleetingly, she wondered why it had taken so long to hear bells when Cooper kissed her.

Abruptly, he broke away, grumbling something unintelligible. He briefly touched his mouth to her cheek before he stood and answered the phone.

CHAPTER 6

"It's Claudia," Cooper said, holding out the receiver.

Ashley stood, her movements awkward as the lingering effects of Cooper's kiss continued to stir her senses. "Hello."

"Ash, I'm sorry," Claudia began. "I didn't know Cooper was going to show up. Is everything okay?"

"Wonderful."

"You two aren't arguing, are you?"

"Quite the contrary," Ashley murmured, closing her eyes as Cooper cupped her cheek with his hand. A kaleidoscope of emotions rippled through her.

"Are the boys down?" Claudia inquired.

"The boys?" Ashley jerked her eyes open and straightened. "Yes, they're both asleep."

"Seth and I may be several hours yet. If everything's peaceful, then don't feel like you need to stay. I'm sure Cooper can handle things if the boys wake up. But they probably won't."

"Okay," she agreed. "I'll talk to you later. Don't worry about anything."

The sound of Claudia's soft laugh came over the line. "I don't think I need to. Take care."

"Bye," Ashley said, and replaced the phone. "That was Claudia checking on the boys," she explained unnecessarily.

"I thought it might be," he said, and nuzzled the top of her head. "Let's finish our dinner," he suggested, taking her by the hand and leading her back to the fireplace.

They ate in contented silence. His look was thoughtful as he paused once to ask, "Do you pray?"

The question was completely unexpected.

"Yes," she responded simply. "What makes you ask?"

He shrugged indifferently, and she had the impression he was far more interested than he wanted to admit. "This is the first time I've eaten pizza on the floor with a beautiful woman."

"Beautiful woman?" she teased. "Where?"

His eyes were more serious than she had ever seen them. "You," he answered, and looked away. The steady tone of his voice revealed how sincere he was.

"There are a lot of things I haven't done

in my life. Prayer is one of them. Tonight when Johnny had me get down on my knees with him . . ." He let the rest of what he was going to say fade. "It felt right." He glanced back at her. "Do you kneel down, too, or is that just something for children?"

"I do on occasion, but it certainly isn't necessary."

Cooper straightened, leaning back against the ottoman. "How do you pray?"

Ashley was surprised by the directness of his question. "Whole books have been written on the subject. I don't know if I'm qualified to answer."

"I didn't ask about anyone else, only you," he countered.

"Well," she began, unsure on how best to answer him. "I don't know that anyone else does it like me."

"I've noted on several occasions that you're a free spirit," he muttered, doing his best to hide his amusement. "Okay, let's go at this from a different angle. When do you pray?"

Answering questions was easier for her. "Mostly in the morning, but any time throughout the day. I pray for little things, parking places at the grocery store, and before I pay bills, and over the mail, and also for the big ones, like everyone in my life staying healthy and happy."

"Why mostly in the morning?" He regarded her steadily.

"That's when I do my devotions," she explained patiently.

"What are devotions?"

"Bible reading and praying," she told him. "My private time with the Lord. My day goes better when I've had a chance to discuss things with Jesus."

"You talk to Him as if He were a regular person?"

"He is," she said, more forcefully than she intended.

He paused and appeared to consider her words thoughtfully. "Do you speak to Him conversationally, then?"

"Yes and no."

"You don't like talking about this, do you?"

"It isn't that," she tried to explain, a soft catch in her voice. "If I tell you . . . I guess I'm afraid you'll think it's silly."

"I won't." The wealth of tenderness in his voice assured her he wouldn't.

"Usually I set aside a formal time for reading my Bible, other devotional books and praying. After I do my Bible reading, I get down on my knees, close my eyes and picture myself on a beautiful beach." She glanced up hesitantly, and Cooper nodded. The warmth in his look seemed to caress her, and she continued. "The scene is perfectly set in my mind. The waves are crashing against the sandy shore and easing back into the sea. I envision the tiny bubbles popping against the sand as the water ebbs out. This is where I meet Christ."

"Does He talk to you?"

"Not with words." She looked away uneasily. "I don't know how to explain this part. I know He hears me, and I know He answers my prayers. I see the evidence of that every day. But as for Him verbally speaking to me, I'd have to say no, though I hear His voice in other ways."

"I don't understand."

"I'm not sure I can explain, I just *do.*"

Cooper seemed to accept that. "Then all you do is talk. You make it sound too easy." He seemed unsure, and she hastened to arrest his doubts.

"No, I spend part of the time thanking Him or . . . praising Him would be a better description, I guess. Another part is spent going over the previous day and asking His forgiveness for any wrongs I've done."

"That shouldn't take a lot of time," he teased.

"Longer than I care to admit," she in-

129

formed him sheepishly and mentally added that the time had increased since she'd been seeing Cooper. "I also keep a list of requests that I pray about regularly and go down each one."

"Am I on your list?" The question was asked so softly that she wasn't sure he'd even spoken.

"Yes," she answered. "I pray for you every day," she admitted, her voice gaining intensity. She didn't add that all the people she loved were on her list. To avoid other questions she continued speaking. "For a while I wrote out my prayers. That was years ago, and it became a journal of God's faithfulness. But I can't write as fast as I can think, so I found that often I'd lose my train of thought. But I've saved those journals and sometimes read over them. When I do, I'm amazed again at God's goodness to me."

A baby's frantic cry broke into their conversation. "Scotty," Ashley said, bounding to her feet. "I'll go see what's wrong."

Scotty was standing in the crib, holding onto the sides. His crying grew louder and more desperate as she hurried into the room.

"What's wrong, Scotty?" she asked soothingly. Soft light from the hallway illuminated the dark recess of the bedroom. She lifted him out of the crib and hugged him close. Checking his diaper, she noted that he didn't seem to be wet. Probably he'd been frightened by a nightmare. Settling him in her arms, she sat in the rocking chair and rocked until she was sure he was back to sleep. With a kiss on the top of his head, she placed him back in his crib.

Cooper was waiting for her at the bottom of the stairs.

"He's asleep again," she whispered.

"I made coffee, would you like a cup?"

She smiled her appreciation. He curved an arm around her narrow waist, bringing her close to his side as he led her back into the den. A silver tea service was set on his desk. She saw that the remains of their dinner had been cleared away, along with their chess game. Biting into her bottom lip to contain her amusement, she decided not to comment on what a neat-freak he was.

He poured the steaming liquid into the china cups, then offered her one. Her hand shook momentarily as she accepted it. Dainty pieces of delicate china made her nervous, and she would have much preferred a ceramic mug.

"This set is lovely," she said, holding the cup in one hand. Tiny pink rosebuds, faded with age, decorated the teacup. She balanced the matching saucer in the palm of her other hand.

"It was my grandmother's," he said proudly. "There are only a few of the original pieces left."

"Oh." Her index finger tightened around the porcelain handle. In her nervousness, her hand wobbled and the boiling hot coffee sloshed over the side onto her hand and her lap, immediately soaking through her thin corduroy jeans. With a gasp of pain, she jumped to her feet. The saucer flew out of her lap and smashed against the leg of the desk, shattering into a thousand pieces.

"Ashley, are you all right?" Cooper bounded to his feet beside her.

Stunned, she couldn't move, her eyes fixed on the broken china as despair filled her. "I'm so sorry," she mumbled. Her voice cracked, and she swallowed past the huge lump building in her throat.

"Forget the china," he said, and took the teacup out of her hand. "It doesn't matter, none of it matters."

"It does matter!" she cried, her voice wobbling uncontrollably. "It matters very much."

"You've got to get that hand in ice water. What about your leg? Is it badly burned?" He tugged at her elbow, almost dragging her into the kitchen. He brought her to the sink and stuck her hand under the cold water. She looked down to see an angry red patch on the back of her left hand, where the coffee had spilled. Funny, she didn't feel any pain. Nothing. Only a horrible deep regret.

"Cooper, please, listen to me. I'm so sorry . . . your grandmother's china is ruined because of me."

"Keep that hand under the water," he said, ignoring her words. Then he went to get ice from the automatic dispenser on the refrigerator door.

Ashley looked away rather than face him. She heard the water splash as he dumped the ice into the sink.

"What about your leg?" he demanded.

"It's fine." She tilted her chin upward and closed her eyes to forestall the tears. The burns didn't hurt; if anything, her hand was growing numb with cold. How could she have been so stupid? His grandmother's china . . . only a few pieces left. His earlier words echoed in her ears until they were nearly deafening.

"Ashley," he whispered, a hand on her shoulder. "Are you all right? You've gone pale. Is the pain very bad? Should I take you to a doctor?"

Talking was impossible, because her throat felt raw and painful, so she shook her head. "Your grandmother's china," she said at last, her voice barely above a tortured whisper.

"Would you quit acting like it's some great tragedy? You've been burned, and that's far more important than some stupid china."

"Do you know what my mother uses for fancy dinners?" she asked in a hoarse voice, then didn't wait for him to answer. "Dishes she picked up at the grocery store. With every ten dollar purchase she could buy another plate at a discount price."

"What has that go to do with anything?" he demanded irritably.

"Nothing. Everything. I swear I'll replace the saucer. I'll contact an antique dealer, I promise. . . ."

"Ashley, stop." His firm hands squeezed her shoulders. "Stop right now. I don't care about a stupid saucer. But I do care about you." His grip tightened. "The saucer means nothing. Nothing," he repeated. "Do you understand?"

Her throat muscles had constricted so that she couldn't speak. Miserably, she hung her head, and her soft curls fell forward, wreathing her face.

She started to tremble, and with a muted

groan Cooper hauled her into his arms.

"Honey, it doesn't matter. Please believe me when I tell you that."

She held on to him hard, because only the warmth of his touch was capable of easing the cold that pierced her heart. A lone tear squeezed past her lashes. She loved Cooper Masters so much it had become a physical pain. Never before had she realized how wrong she was for him. He needed someone who . . .

She wasn't allowed to complete the thought as Cooper's hand touched her face, turning her to meet his gaze. Her tortured eyes tried to avoid him, but he held her steady.

"Ashley, look at me." He sounded gruff, impatient.

But she was determined, and she shook herself loose, then swayed against him, her fingers spread against his shirt. He found her lips and kissed her with a desperation she hadn't experienced from him. It was as if he needed to confirm what he was saying, to comfort her, reassure her. She knew she shouldn't accept any of it. But one minute in Cooper's arms and it didn't matter. All she could do was feel.

His hands roamed her back as he buried his face in the hair at the side of her face.

"Let's sit down."

He took her into the living room and set her down in the soft comfort of the large sofa. Next he opened the drapes and revealed the same view of Puget Sound that they'd enjoyed on Thanksgiving Day, when they'd walked on his property in the rain.

Hands in his pockets, he paused to admire the beauty. "Sometimes in the evening I sit here, staring into the sky, counting the stars." He spoke absently, standing at the far corner of the window, gazing into the still night. "Looking at all that magnificence makes me feel small and very insignificant. One man, alone." His back was to her. "It's times like this that make me regret not having a wife and family. I've worked hard, and what do I have to show for it? An expensive home and no one to share it with." He stopped and turned, their eyes meeting. For a breathless moment they stared at one another. Then he dropped his gaze and turned slowly back to the window.

Confused for a moment, she watched as he turned away from her, as if trying to block her out of his mind. His action troubled her. He stood alone, across the room, a solitary figure silhouetted against the night. What was he telling her? She didn't understand, but she did realize that he had revealed a part of himself others didn't see.

Unfolding her long legs from the sofa, she joined him at the window. Standing at his side, she slipped an arm around his waist as if she'd done it a thousand times.

He smiled at her then, and she couldn't remember ever seeing anything transform a face more. His dark eyes seemed to spark with something she couldn't define. Happiness? Contentment? Pleasure? His smile widened as he looped his arm over her shoulders, and then he brushed her temple with a light kiss.

"Do you have your Christmas tree up yet?"

"No," she whispered, afraid talking normally would destroy the wonderful mood. "I thought I'd put it up tomorrow."

"Would you like some help?"

The offer shocked her. "I'd . . . I'd love some."

"What time?"

"Probably afternoon." Her sigh was filled with a sense of dread. "I've got to get some shopping done. There are only a few days left, and I've hardly started."

"Me either, and I still need to get something for the boys."

"I'm afraid I haven't had the chance to

shop. The last days of school were so hectic. I hate leaving everything to the last minute like this."

"Why don't we make a day of it?" he suggested. "I'll pick you up, say around ten. We can do the shopping, go for lunch and decorate your tree afterward."

"That sounds wonderful. I'd like that. I'd like it very much."

"And, Ashley . . ." Cooper said, looking away uncomfortably.

"Yes?"

"I was thinking about buying myself a pair of cowboy boots and wanted to ask your advice about the best place to go."

"I know just the store, in the Pavilion near Southcenter. But be warned, they're expensive." As soon as the words were out, she regretted them. Cooper didn't need to worry about money.

He chuckled and gave her a tiny squeeze. "I wish other people were as reluctant to spend my money."

"We'll see how reluctant I am tomorrow," she murmured with a small laugh.

CHAPTER 7

Ashley changed clothes three times before the doorbell chimed, announcing Cooper's arrival. Her final choice had been a soft gray wool skirt and a white bouclé-knit sweater. The outfit, with knee-high black leather boots, was one she usually reserved for church, but she wanted everything to be perfect for Cooper.

A warm smile lit up her face as she opened the door. "Morning, you're right on . . ." She didn't finish; the words died on her lips. Cooper in jeans! Levis so new and stiff they looked as if they would stand up on their own. Her lashes fluttered downward to disguise her shock.

"Morning. You look as beautiful as ever."

"Thank you," she whispered, somewhat bewildered. "Do you want a cup of coffee or something before we go?"

"No, I think we'd better get started before the crowds get too bad."

She lounged back in her seat, content to let him drive. He flipped a switch, and immediately the interior was filled with classical music. She savored the gentle sounds of the string section and glanced up, surprised when the music abruptly changed to a top forty station.

"Why'd you do that?" she asked, her blue gaze sweeping toward him, searching his profile.

"I thought this would probably be more to your liking." His gaze remained on the freeway, the traffic surprisingly heavy for early morning.

"It's not," she murmured, a little of her earlier happiness dissipating with the thought that Cooper assumed she preferred more popular music to the classics. *But don't you?* her mind countered.

They took the exit for Southcenter, a huge shopping complex south of Seattle, but didn't stop there. The area's largest toy store was situated nearby, and they had decided earlier that it would be the best place to start.

The parking lot was already full, so Cooper had to drive around a couple of times before locating a spot at the far end.

His hand cupped her elbow as they hurried inside. Only a few shopping carts were left, and she glanced around, doing her best to squelch a growing sense of panic. The store had barely opened, and already there was hardly room to move through the aisles.

"My goodness," she murmured impatiently. They were forced to wait to move past the throng of shoppers entering the first aisle. "Do you want to come back later?" she asked, glancing at him anxiously.

"I don't think it's going to get any better," he muttered darkly.

"I don't think it will, either. Maybe we should decide now what we want to buy the boys. That would at least streamline the process. We're going together, aren't we?" At Cooper's questioning glance, she added, "I mean, we'll split the cost."

"I'll pay," he insisted.

"Cooper," she groaned. "Either we divide the cost or forget it."

His mouth thinned slightly. "All right, I should know better. You and that pride of yours."

He looked as if he wanted to add something more, but the crowd moved, and she pushed the cart forward.

"Okay, what should we get Johnny?" Her eyes followed the floor-to-ceiling display of computer games. On the other side of the aisle were more traditional games and puzzles.

"I've thought of something perfect," Cooper announced proudly. "I'm sure you'll agree."

"What?"

"A computer chess game. I saw one advertised the other day."

"He's too young for that," Ashley declared. She hated to stifle Cooper's enthusiasm, but Johnny wasn't interested in chess.

"He's not," Cooper shot back. "I've been teaching him a few moves. It's the perfect gift — educational, too."

"Good," she said emphatically. "Then you get him that, but I want to buy him something he'll enjoy."

Cooper's soft chuckle caught her unaware. "What's so funny?" she asked.

"You." He paused and looked around before lightly kissing her cheek. "I can't think of a thing in the world that you and I will ever agree on. Our tastes are too different." His gaze seemed to be fixed on her softly parted lips. "Do men often have to restrain themselves from kissing you?"

A happy light shimmered from her deep blue eyes. "Hundreds," she teased. Immediately she realized it had been the wrong thing to say. She could almost visualize the

142

wall that was going up between them.

He straightened and pretended an interest in one of the displays.

"Cooper," she whispered, and laid her hand across his forearm. "That was a dumb joke."

"I imagine it was closer to the truth than you realize."

"Oh, hardly," she denied with a light laugh.

An hour and a half later, their packages stored in the booth beside them, Ashley exhaled a long sigh.

"Coffee," Cooper told the waitress, who quickly returned and filled their mugs.

"I can't remember a time when I needed this more," Ashley murmured and took an appreciative sip.

"Me, either. Could you believe that checkout line?"

"But Johnny's going to love his fire truck and hat."

"And his computer chess game."

"Of course," she agreed, grinning.

"At least we agreed on Scotty's gift. That wasn't so difficult, was it?"

Ashley's gaze skipped from Cooper to the stuffed animal beside him, and she burst into peals of laughter. "Oh, Cooper, if only your friends could see you now with that gorilla next to you."

"Yes, I guess that would be cause for amusement."

Digging through her purse, Ashley brought out her Bible, flipping through the worn pages.

"What are you doing now?" he asked in a hushed whisper.

"Don't worry, I'm not going to stand on the seat and start a crusade. I want to find something."

"What?"

"A verse." She paused, a finger marking the place. "Here it is. First Peter 1:4."

"Honestly, you've got to be the only woman in the world who whips out her Bible in a restaurant."

Unaffected by his teasing tone, she laid the book open on the tabletop, turned it sideways and pointed to the passage she wanted him to read. "After what we just went through, I decided I wanted to be sure heaven has reserved seating. It does, look." Aloud she read a portion of the text. " 'To obtain an inheritance which is reserved in heaven for you.' "

A hint of a smile quivered at the edges of his mouth. "You're serious, aren't you?"

"Sure I am. I've seen pictures of riots that

looked more organized than that mess we were in."

He laughed loudly then, attracting the curious glances of others. "Ashley Robbins, I find you delightful."

Pleased, she beamed and placed the small Bible back inside her purse.

"Where do you want to go next?" he asked as he glanced at his wristwatch.

"Do you need to be back for something?"

He raised his eyes to meet hers. "No," he said, and shook his head to emphasize his denial.

"If you feel like you could brave the maddening crowd a second time, we could tackle the mall."

He looked unsure for a moment. She couldn't blame him. The thought of facing thousands of last-minute shoppers wasn't an appealing one, but she did still have gifts to buy — and he wanted those boots.

"Sure, why not?" he agreed.

Ashley could think of forty thousand hectic reasons why not, but she didn't voice a single one, content simply being with Cooper.

"However, I hope you don't object if we store Tarzan's friend in the trunk of the car," he added, and glanced wryly at the stuffed animal.

The crowds at the mall proved to be even worse than the toy store, but a couple of hours later, their arms loaded with packages, they finally retreated to the car.

Even Cooper, who was normally so calm and reserved, looked a bit ashen after fighting the chaos. They hadn't even stopped for lunch, eating caramel apples instead as they walked from one end of the mall to the other.

"Do you think Claudia will like the necklace?" he asked as he joined her in the front seat and inserted the key into the ignition.

"Of course." Ashley had picked out the turquoise necklace and knew her friend would love it, but he was still skeptical. "Trust me."

"There's something about that phrase that makes me nervous."

"But you didn't buy two. Now I'm curious," she ventured, not paying attention to what he'd said.

"Two? Two what?"

"Necklaces." She gave him an impatient look. Sometimes they seemed to be speaking at complete cross purposes.

"Do you think Claudia would want two?" He gave her a curious glance.

"Of course not," she said with a sigh. "But you always buy me the same thing as Claudia." She didn't add that it had been perfume for the past three Christmases.

"Not this year."

"Really?" Her interested piqued, she asked, "What are you getting me?"

"Like John and Scott, you'll have to wait until Christmas morning."

She was more pleased than she dared show. Not that she would be forced to wait until Christmas, but that she'd moved beyond the same safe category as Claudia. It thrilled her to know that their relationship had evolved to the point that he wanted to get her something different this year.

Cooper played with the radio until he found some Christmas music.

Again Ashley could feel the comforting music float around her, soothing her tattered nerves. "Doesn't that make you want to sing?"

"Every time you say that we have a storm," he complained.

"Killjoy," she muttered under her breath.

A large hand reached over and squeezed hers. "Ready to decorate the tree?"

"More than ready," she agreed. Much of her shopping remained to be done, but she'd promised Claudia that they would head out early Monday morning so there would be plenty of time to finish.

The remainder of the short drive to her apartment was accomplished in a companionable silence. Her mind wandered to the first time Cooper had asked her to dinner after she'd paid off the loan. At the time she would have doubted she could ever sit at his side without being nervous. Now she felt relaxed, content.

Although nothing had ever been openly stated, their relationship had come a long way in the past couple of months. She could only pray that this budding rapport would continue after Claudia, Seth and the boys returned to Alaska.

Ever the gentleman, Cooper took the apartment key away from her and unlocked the door. Men didn't usually do that sort of thing for her, but then again, she probably wouldn't have let anyone but Cooper.

"I put the tree on the lanai until it was time to decorate," she told him, and took his coat, hanging it with hers in the closet. When she turned around Cooper was helping himself to a handful of popcorn.

"I wouldn't eat that if I were you, it's a week old."

He dropped the kernels back into the bowl and wrinkled his nose.

"Quite giving me funny looks like I'm a

terrible housekeeper. You're supposed to leave the popcorn out to get stale. It strings easier that way."

"Strings?"

"For the tree."

"Of course, for the tree," he echoed.

She had the uneasy sensation that he didn't know what she meant. Lightly, she shrugged her shoulders. He would learn soon enough.

"Are you hungry?" she asked on her way into the kitchen. "I can make us pastrami sandwiches with dill pickles and potato chips."

"That sounds good, except I'll have my potato chips on the side."

"Cute," she murmured, sticking her head around the corner.

"With you I never know," he complained with a full smile.

While she made lunch, Cooper brought the Christmas tree inside. Since it was already in the stand, all he had to do was find a place to set it in the living room. When he'd finished he joined her in the compact kitchen.

Working contentedly with her back to him, she hummed softly and cut thin slices of pickle.

"You can have one of the chocolates I

bought if you like," she told him, as she spread a thick layer of mustard across the bread.

"I thought you said chocolates weren't meant to be shared."

She laughed softly. "I was only teasing."

"Ashley . . ."

Just the way he spoke her name caused her to pause and turn around.

"I think we should do this before we eat."

"Do what?" Her heart was chugging like a locomotive at the look he was giving her.

"This." He took the knife out of her hand and laid it on the counter. His gaze centered on her mouth.

She gave a soft welcoming moan as his lips fit over hers. All day she'd yearned for his touch. It was torture to be so close to him and maintain the friendly facade, when in her heart all she wanted was to be held and loved by him.

When he dragged his mouth from hers, she knew he felt as unsatisfied as she did. Kissing was quickly becoming insufficient to satisfy either of them. His hands roamed possessively over her back, arching her closer. Again his mouth dipped to drink from the sweetness of hers. With a shuddering breath he released her.

Sensation after sensation swirled through

150

her. These feelings he stirred within her were what God had intended her to feel toward the man she loved, and she couldn't doubt the rightness of them. But what was *he* feeling? Certainly he wasn't immune to all this.

His smile was gentle when he asked, "Did you say something about lunch?"

"Lunch," she repeated like a robot, then lightly shook her head, irritated that she was reacting like a lovesick teenager. No, she mused, Cooper couldn't help but be aware of the powerful physical attraction between them. He was simply much more in control of himself than she was.

A few minutes later she carried their meal into the living room on a tray. He was sorting through her ornaments and looked up. A frown was creasing his brow.

"What's wrong?" she asked, setting their plates on the coffee table and glancing over at him.

"There's something written across these glass ornaments."

"I know," she answered simply.

"But what is it and why?"

A soft smile touched her mouth as she lifted half of her sandwich and prepared to take the first bite. "Remember how I mentioned that I dated the man who sold me

Milligan a couple of times?"

"I remember."

The tightness in his voice sent her searching gaze to him a second time. "Unfortunately, Jim was decidedly not a Christian. We saw one another a couple of times in December, and he couldn't understand why I didn't want to do certain things."

"What things?" Cooper's tone had taken on an arctic chill.

"It doesn't matter," she said, and smiled, dismissing his curiosity. The past was over, and she didn't want to review it with him. "But one thing I *am* grateful for is the fact Jim told me the Christmas tree is a pagan custom. He found it interesting that I professed this deep faith in Christ yet chose to allow a pagan ritual to desecrate my home." She set the sandwich aside and knelt beside Cooper on the carpet. "You know, he's right. I was shocked, so I decided to make my Christmas tree Christ centered."

"But how?"

"It wasn't that difficult. The tree is an evergreen, constant, never changing, just as my faith in Christ is meant to be. And Christ died upon a tree. The lights were the easiest part. Jesus asks that each one of us be the light of the world. But when it came to the ornaments, I had to be a little inventive, so I took glitter glue —"

"Glitter glue?" he interrupted.

"Glue that has glitter already in it. It's much easier to write out the fruits of the Holy Spirit that way."

"Hold on, you've lost me."

"Here." She stood and retrieved her Bible from the oak end table. Flipping the pages, she located the verses she wanted. "Paul wrote in his epistle to the Galatians about the fruits of the Christian life."

"Love, joy, peace," he read from each of the pink glass ornaments. "I get it now."

"Exactly," she stated excitedly.

"Clever girl." His thick brows arched expressively.

"Thank you."

"I'm very curious now about how you tie in the popcorn."

"Yes, well . . ." Frantically, her mind searched for a plausible reason. She hadn't thought about the decorative strings she added each year.

"I've got it," he said. "White and spotless like the Christ child."

"Very good," she congratulated him.

There was a disconcerted look in his eyes as they met hers. "Your commitment to Christ is important to you, isn't it?"

"Vital," she confirmed. "One's relationship with God is a personal thing. But Christ is the most important person in my life. He has been for several years."

"You stopped seeing Madigan because he didn't have the same belief system as you."

"More or less. In some ways we hit it off immediately. I liked Jim, I still do. But our relationship was headed for a dead end, so I cut it off before either one of us got serious."

"Because he didn't believe the same way as you? Isn't that narrow minded?"

"To me it isn't, and that wasn't the only reason. Cooper . . ." She paused and held her breath when she saw his troubled look. "Why all the questions? Do you think I'm wrong in the way I believe?"

"It doesn't matter what I think."

"Of course, it matters." *Because you do,* she added silently.

He rose and walked to the far side of the room. "I don't believe the same way you do. Oh, I acknowledge there's a God. I couldn't look at the heavens and examine our world and not believe in a Supreme Being. I accept that Christ was born, but I never have understood salvation, justification and all the rest of it. Everyone talks about the free gift, but —"

A loud knock on her door interrupted him.

She glanced at him and shrugged. She wasn't expecting anyone. She got to her feet, crossed the room and checked the peephole.

"It's Webb," she told Cooper before opening the door.

"Hello, Sweet Thing. How's your day been?" He sauntered into the room whistling "White Christmas" and paused long enough to brush his lips across her cheek. The song died on his lips when he spotted Cooper.

"Webb," Ashley said stiffly, folding her hands tightly together in front of her. "This is Cooper Masters. I believe I've mentioned him."

She watched as the two men exchanged handshakes. "Cooper, this is Dennis Webb."

Ashley wanted to shout at her friend. Webb couldn't have picked a worse time to pop in for one of his spontaneous visits.

"No, I can't say that I recall you mentioning him," Webb announced as he glanced back to Ashley.

She seethed silently and somehow managed a weak smile.

"I can't say the same about you," Cooper muttered in the stiff, formal tone she'd come to hate.

"Would you like to sit down, Webb?" She motioned toward the sofa and glared at him, desperately hoping he would get the message and leave.

"Thanks." He plopped down on the couch and crossed his legs. "You missed a great party last night. Hardly seemed right without you there, Ash. Next time I won't take no for an answer."

Cooper lowered himself onto the far end of the sofa. His back remained rigid.

"I'll make coffee," Ashley volunteered as she left the room, thinking the atmosphere back there was so thick she could taste it.

"I'll see if I can help in the kitchen," she heard Webb say, and a second later he was at her side.

"Who is this guy?" he hissed.

"What do you mean?" she demanded in a hushed whisper, then didn't wait for an answer. "He's my best friend's uncle, and what do you mean I've never mentioned him? I talk about him all the time."

"You haven't," Webb insisted. "Unless he's the one you played chess with and lost?"

"That's him." Her fingers refused to work properly, and coffee grounds spilled across the counter. "Darn, darn, darn."

"I don't care who he is, if he calls me Webber one more time, I'm going to punch him."

"Webb," she expelled her breath and noticed that Cooper was watching her intently from the doorway. She stopped talking and forced a beguiling smile onto her face. Her teeth were clenched so tight her jaw hurt. "Can't you see it's not a good time?" she hissed beneath her breath.

"Are you saying you want me to leave?"

"Yes." She nearly shouted the one word.

Cooper stepped closer. "Is everything all right, Ashley?" he asked in a formal tone, but his burning gaze was focused on Webb.

The look was searing. She had never seen such disapproval illuminated so clearly on anyone's features. Cooper's mouth was pinched, his eyes narrowed. For a crazy second she wanted to laugh. The two men were eyeing one another like bears who had encroached on each other's territory.

"I'm fine. Webb was just saying that he has to go."

"I do?" he said. "Oh, yes, I guess I do." He walked out of the kitchen with Ashley on his heels. "I'll talk to you soon," he told her, his gaze full of meaning.

"Right." She held open the door for him. "Sorry you have to leave so soon."

The look Webb gave her nearly sent her

into peals of laughter. "I'll phone you soon," she promised.

"Nice meeting you, Cooper," Webb said graciously. "Now that I recall, Ash *has* mentioned you. I understand you play a mean game of chess."

"I play," Cooper admitted with a look of indifference.

"I dabble in the game myself," Webb said, tossing Ashley a teasing glance.

"See you later, Webb," she said firmly, and closed the door. The lock clicked shut, and she paused, her eyes closed, and released a long, slow, breath.

"Nice fellow, Webber," Cooper said from behind her.

"He's a friend." She had to be certain Cooper understood that her relationship with Webb didn't go any further than that of congenial co-workers.

"I imagine he's the kind of Christian who fits right into that cozy picture you have built in your mind." His tone was almost harsh.

Ashley did her best to ignore it. "Webb's a wonderful Christian man."

"You probably should marry someone like him," he stated with a sharp edge. His gaze narrowed on her. It wasn't difficult to tell that he was angry, but she didn't know why.

"You're upset, aren't you?" she asked, confronting him. Her back was against the door, her hands clenched at her side.

Cooper's long strides carried him to the far side of the room. He tried to ram his hands in his pockets, apparently forgetting he was wearing jeans. That seemed to irritate him all the more.

"We never did eat our lunch," she said shakily.

He glared at the thick sandwich and then back to her. "I'm not hungry."

"Let's decorate the tree, then." She hugged her middle to ward off the cold she felt beginning to surround her. Cooper was freezing her out, and she didn't know what to say or do to prevent him from doing that.

He stared at her blankly, as if he hadn't heard a word she'd said. Helplessly, she watched as he opened the closet door and took out his coat.

"Cooper?" she whispered, but he didn't hesitate, slipping his arms into the sleeves and starting on the buttons.

She was still standing in front of the door, and she decided she wouldn't move, wouldn't let him walk out as if she wasn't there. What had happened? Everything had been so beautiful last night and today, and now, for no apparent reason, he was pushing her away. She felt as if their relationship had taken a giant step backward.

His drawn expression didn't alter as he came to stand directly in front of her. His hand brushed a blond curl off her face and lingered a second to trace a finger across her cheek.

"You really should marry someone like Webber."

"No." The sound was barely audible. "I won't." How could she marry Webb when she loved Cooper?

"Funny how we never seem to do the things we should," he muttered cryptically.

"Cooper?" Her voice throbbed with a feeling she couldn't identify. Agony? Need? Desperation? "What's wrong?" she tried again.

"Other than the fact you and I are as different as night and day?"

"We've always been different, why should it matter now?"

"I don't know," he told her honestly.

"I had a wonderful time today," she whispered, and hung her head to avoid his searching look. Her lashes fluttered wearily. She knew she was losing, but not why. "I don't want it to end like this. I didn't know Webb was coming."

"It isn't Webber," Cooper admitted

harshly. "It's everything." An ominous silence followed his announcement. "I like to pretend with you."

"Pretend?" She lifted her gaze, uncertain of what he was admitting.

"You're warm and alive, and you make me yearn for things that were never meant to be."

"Now you're talking in riddles. And I hate riddles, because I can never understand them. I don't understand *you.*"

"No," he murmured, and rubbed a hand across his face. "I don't suppose that's possible."

Ashley didn't know what directed her, perhaps instinct. Of their own volition her arms slipped around his neck. At first he held himself stiff and unyielding against her, but she refused to be deterred. Her exploring fingers toyed with the dark hair at the back of his head. She applied a gentle pressure, urging his mouth to hers. His resistance grew stronger, forcing her to stand on her tip toes and mold herself to him. Gradually, she eased her mouth over his.

He didn't want her kiss, but she could feel the part of him that unwillingly reached out to her.

Abruptly he broke the contact and pulled himself away. Both hands cupped her face, tilting it up at an angle. A smoldering light of something she couldn't decipher burned in his eyes.

"Ashley." The husky tone of his voice betrayed his desire, yet she marveled at his control.

"Hmm?" she answered with a contented whisper.

"Next time I start acting like a jerk, promise me you'll bring me out of my ill temper just like this."

She gave a glad cry and kissed him again. "I promise," she said after a long while.

CHAPTER 8

"Was Cooper with you Saturday?" Claudia asked as she laid the menu aside.

Most of Monday morning and half the afternoon had been spent finishing up their Christmas shopping. For the past two hours Ashley had dragged Claudia to every antique store she could find.

Her index finger made a lazy circle around the rim of her water glass. "What makes you ask?" A peculiar pain knotted her stomach. It happened every time she suspected Cooper didn't want anyone to know they were seeing one another. She had spent the entire day with him. After decorating the tree they'd gone out to dinner and a movie. It was midnight before he kissed her good night. Yet he hadn't told Claudia anything.

"What makes me ask?" Claudia repeated incredulously. "You mean besides the fact that he mysteriously disappeared for the entire day? Then he saunters in about midnight with a sheepish look. Gets up early Sunday morning whistling. Cooper. Whistling. He even went to church with us again, which surprised both Seth and me."

"What makes you think I had anything to do with it?"

"What is it with you two? You'd think you were ashamed to be seen with one another."

"You're being ridiculous."

"I'm not. Look at how elusive you're being. Were you or were you not with Cooper Sunday?"

"Yes, I was with him."

"Just part of the time?"

"No," she admitted and breathed in heavily. "All day."

"Ash?" Claudia hesitated as if searching for the right words. "I know you're probably going to say this is none of my business, but I've never seen you act like this."

"Act like what?" she returned defensively.

"All our lives you were the fearless one. There didn't seem to be anything you weren't willing to try. I've never seen you so reticent."

Ashley shrugged one shoulder slightly.

"You're in love with Cooper, aren't you?"

A small smile played over Ashley's mouth. "Yes." It felt good to finally verbalize her feelings. "Very much."

Claudia's eyes glinted with an inner glow of happiness. "Who would ever have guessed you'd fall in love with Cooper?"

"I don't know. Probably no one."

"Has he told you he loves you yet?" Claudia asked, obviously doing her best to contain her excitement.

"No, but then I'm not exactly an 'uptown girl,' am I?" The words slipped out more flippantly than she'd intended.

"Ashley," Claudia snapped, "I can't believe you'd say something like that. You're closer to me than any sister could ever —"

"It's not you," Ashley interrupted, lowering her gaze to her half-full water glass. "Cooper's ashamed to be seen with me."

"That's pure nonsense," Claudia insisted.

"I wish it was," Ashley said in a serious tone.

Any additional discussion was interrupted by the waitress, who arrived to take their order.

"Promise me one thing," Claudia asked as soon as the woman was gone, her eyes pleading.

"What?"

"That you won't drag me to any more antique shops. Cooper doesn't care about that saucer, so I don't see why you should."

"But I do," Ashley said forcefully. "I'm

going to replace it if I have to look for the rest of my life."

"Honestly, Ash, it's not that big a deal. Cooper would feel terrible if he knew the trouble you're putting yourself through."

"Don't you dare tell him."

Their Cobb salads arrived, and the flow of conversation came to a halt as they began to eat.

"You're planning to come with us Wednesday, aren't you?" Claudia asked, looking up from her salad.

"Is that the day you're taking the boys to Seattle Center Enchanted Forest?" Every Christmas the Food Circus inside the Center created a fantasyland for young children. The large open area was filled with tall trees and a train that enthralled the youngsters. Clowns performed and handed out balloons. "That's Christmas Eve day."

"Brilliant deduction," Claudia teased. "Cooper's going," she added, as if Ashley needed an inducement.

Ashley's blond curls bounced as she laughed. "I'd be excited about it even if Cooper wasn't coming along. We're going to have a wonderful time. The boys will love it."

"Cooper's been asking Seth a lot of questions," Claudia announced unexpectedly.

"Questions? About what?"

"The Bible." Claudia placed her fork beside her plate. "They spent almost the entire afternoon on Sunday discussing things. When I talked to Seth about it later, he told me that he felt inadequate because some of Cooper's questions were so complicated. Personally, I don't know where Cooper stands with the Lord, but he seems to be having a difficult time with some of the basic concepts." She paused, then added, "He can't seem to accept that salvation is not something we can earn with donations or good works."

"I can understand that," Ashley defended him. "Cooper has worked hard all his life. Nothing's been free. I can see that the concept would be more difficult for him to accept than for others."

Claudia lounged back, a smile twinkling in her eyes. "You really *do* love him, don't you?"

"I'll tell you something else that'll shock you." Ashley nervously smoothed her pant leg. "I've loved him from the time I was sixteen. It's just been . . . harder to hide lately."

Claudia's expression softened knowingly. "I think I guessed how you felt almost as soon as I saw the two of you together at the

167

airport when Seth and I arrived with the boys. And then, when I thought back, I realized how long it had been going on, at least for you."

"How did you know?" Ashley's eyes narrowed thoughtfully.

"From the time we were teens, it was you who defended Cooper when he did something to irritate me. You were always ready to leap to his defense."

"Was I so obvious?"

"Not at all," Claudia assured her. "Now, are you ready for something else?" She didn't wait for a response. "Cooper's been in love with you since before I married Seth."

"That I don't believe," Ashley argued. She picked up her fork and put it back down twice before finally setting it aside.

"Think about it," Claudia challenged, a determined lift to her chin. "Seth asked me to marry him, and I was so undecided. I knew I loved him, but moving to Alaska, leaving school and all my dreams of becoming a doctor, made the decision difficult. You were telling me to follow my heart, and at the same time Cooper was unconditionally opposed to the whole idea."

"I remember how miserable you were."

"I was more than miserable. I was at the

airport wanting to die, I loved him so much, yet I felt it would never work for Seth and me. You told me if I loved him to go after him." Her blue eyes glimmered with the memory, and a soft smile played at the corners of her mouth. "Still, I was undecided, and I looked to Cooper, wanting him to make up my mind for me. It's funny how clearly I can recall that scene now. Cooper glanced from me to you. At the time I didn't recognize the look in his eyes, but I do now. After so many bitter arguments, Cooper looked at you and told me the decision was mine."

"I think you've blown the whole thing out of proportion." Ashley felt safer in denying what her friend thought than placing any faith in it.

"Don't you see?" Claudia persisted. "Cooper changed his mind because, for the first time in his life, he knew what it was to be in love with someone."

"I wish it were true," Ashley murmured sadly, "but if he felt that way four years ago, why didn't he make an effort to go out with me?"

A wayward lock of auburn hair fell across Claudia's cheek. "Knowing Cooper, that isn't so difficult to understand."

"I wish I could believe it, I really do."

Claudia reached across the small table and squeezed Ashley's forearm. "I've been waiting four years to give you the kind of advice you gave me. Go for him, Ash. Cooper needs you."

Ashley's eyes were filled with determination. "I have no intention of letting him go."

Claudia's laugh was almost musical. "In some ways I almost pity my uncle."

Ashley was sitting on the floor with Scott on her lap when Johnny crawled in beside him. "Can we play a game, Auntie Ash?"

Ashley looked into his round blue eyes, unsure. She'd told Claudia she'd watch the boys while her friends wrapped Christmas presents, and she didn't want to get Johnny all wound up.

"What kind of game?"

"Horsey. Uncle Cooper let me ride him, and Scotty and Daddy were the other horsey."

The picture that flashed into her mind produced a warm smile. "But I wouldn't be a good horse for both you *and* Scotty," she told him gently.

A disappointed look clouded his expressive face, but he accepted her decision. "Can you read?" he asked next, and handed her a book.

"Sure." With her natural flair for theatrics, she began to read from the *Bible Story Book*.

"How many days until Jesus's birthday?" Johnny asked when she'd finished.

"Only a few now. Are you excited to open all your presents?"

Eagerly he shook his head. "If Jesus hadn't been born, would we have Christmas?" He cocked his head at a curious angle so he could look at her.

"No. We wouldn't have any churches or Sunday School, either."

"What else wouldn't we have?"

"If Jesus hadn't come, our world would be a very sad place. Because Jesus wouldn't live in people's hearts, and they wouldn't love one another the way they should."

"We wouldn't have a Christmas tree," Johnny added.

"Or presents, or Easter."

The young boy's eyes grew wide. "Not even Easter?"

"Nope."

Johnny sat quietly for a minute. "Then the best gift of all at Christmas is Jesus."

A rush of tenderness warmed Ashley's heart. "You said it beautifully."

Scotty squirmed out of her arms and onto the thick carpet, crawling with all his might toward the Christmas tree. Ashley hurriedly intercepted him and, with a laugh, swept him from the carpet and into the air high above her head.

Scotty gurgled with delight. "You like this funny looking tree, don't you?" she asked him, laughing. "I bet if you got the opportunity, every present here would be torn to shreds."

The front door closed, and she turned with Scotty in her arms to find Cooper shaking the rain from his hat.

"Hi."

He didn't see her immediately, and as he turned a surprised look crossed his dark features. Almost as quickly the look was replaced with one of welcome that sent her heart beating at an erratic pace.

"Claudia and Seth left you to the mercies of these two again?"

"No, they're wrapping presents. My duty is to keep the boys out of trouble."

He hung his coat in the hall closet and joined her, lifting Johnny into his arms. The boy squeezed Cooper's neck and gave him a moist kiss on the cheek.

"You know what Auntie Ash said?" John leaned back to look at his uncle.

"I can only guess," Cooper replied, his eyes brightening with a smile. Lovingly he searched her face.

"She said if Jesus hadn't been born, we wouldn't have Christmas."

"No, we wouldn't," Cooper agreed.

"I know something else we wouldn't have," she murmured and moistened her lips.

Johnny's gaze followed hers, and he shouted excitedly, "Mistletoe."

Cooper's eyes hadn't left hers, although his narrowed slightly as if he couldn't take them off her.

"Mistletoe," she repeated, her invitation blatant.

Motionless, Cooper held her look, but gave her no indication of what he was thinking.

Two quick strides carried him to her side. Her senses whirled as he placed Johnny on the ground and gathered her in his arms. Half of her pleasure came from the fact that he didn't look around to see if anyone was watching.

Cooper's gaze skidded to the baby she was still holding between them, and he let out a long exaggerated sigh. "No help for this. I can't kiss you properly while you're holding the baby."

"I'll take a rain check," she teased.

"But I won't," he announced, then removed Scotty from her arms and gently set him on the floor.

Ashley started to protest, but before she could utter a sound, Cooper's mouth was over hers. Winding her arms around his neck, she reveled in the feel of him as his hands gripped her narrow waist.

The sound of someone clearing their throat had barely registered with her when he abruptly broke off the kiss and breathed in deeply.

"You two forget something?" Claudia demanded, hands on her hips as she watched them with a teasing smile.

"Forget?" Ashley was still caught in the rapture; clear thinking was almost impossible. Cooper's warm breath continued to caress her cheek, and she knew he was as affected as she was.

"Like Scotty and John?"

"Oh." Ashley gasped and looked around, remembering how the baby had been enthralled with the Christmas tree.

Seth had lifted the baby by the seat of his pants and was holding him several inches off the ground.

"I think we've been found out," Ashley whispered to Cooper.

"Looks that way," he said releasing her.

Seth handed his wife the baby, who cooed happily, and the two men left the room.

"I've been meaning to ask you all day what you're wearing tomorrow," Claudia said, tucking her son close to her side.

"Wearing tomorrow?" Ashley echoed. "I don't understand?"

"To the party." Claudia looked at her as if she had suddenly developed amnesia.

"The party?"

"Cooper's dinner party tomorrow night, of course," Claudia said, laughing lightly.

The world suddenly seemed to come to an abrupt stop. Ashley's heart pounded frantically; the blood rushed to her face. In that instant she knew what it must feel like to be hit in the stomach. Claudia continued to elaborate, giving her the details of the formal dinner party. But Ashley was only half listening; the words drifted off into nothingness. The only sound that penetrated the cloud of hurt and disappointment were the words *family . . . friends.* She was neither. She was the cook's daughter, nothing more.

She heard footsteps, and her breathing became actively painful as her gaze shifted to meet Cooper's eyes. Standing there, Ashley prayed she would find something in his look that could explain why she had been excluded from the party. But all she saw was regret. He hadn't wanted her to know.

"Ashley, are those tears?" Claudia asked

in a shocked whisper. "What did I say? What's wrong?"

In a haze, Ashley looked beyond the concerned face of her friend. Seth was standing with Johnny at his side, a troubled look on his face. Everyone she loved was there to witness her humiliation. Without a word, she turned and walked out of the house.

"Ashley." There was a pleading quality in Cooper's voice as he followed her out of the house. She quickened her pace, ignoring his demand that she wait. By the time he reached her, she was inside her car, the key in the ignition.

"Will you stop?" he shouted, his mouth tight. "At least give me the chance to explain."

Nothing was worth her staying and listening; he'd said everything without having uttered a word. She wanted to tell him that, but it was all she could do to swallow back the tears.

When she started the engine, Cooper tried to yank open the car door, but she was quicker and hit the lock. Jerking the car into reverse, she pulled out of the driveway. One last glance in Cooper's direction showed him standing alone, watching her leave. His shoulders were hunched in defeat.

Her cell phone was ringing even before she reached her small apartment. She knew without looking that it was Cooper. She also knew he would refuse to give up, so finally, in exasperation, she answered.

"Yes," she snapped.

A slight pause followed. "Miss Robbins?"

"Yes?" Some of the impatience left her voice.

"This is Larry Marshall, of Marshall's Antiques. You talked to me this morning about that china saucer you were looking for."

"Did you find one?"

"A friend of mine has the piece you're looking for," he told her.

"How soon can I pick it up?"

"Tomorrow, if you like. There's only one problem," he continued.

"What's that?"

"My friend's shop is in Victoria, Canada."

Ashley wouldn't have cared if it was in Alaska. Replacing Cooper's china saucer was of the utmost importance. He need never know it had come from her. She could give it to Claudia. After writing down the dealer's name and address, she thanked the man and told him she would put a check in the mail to cover his finder's fee.

Immediately after she replaced the receiver, the phone rang again. She stared at it dumbfounded, unable to move as Cooper's name came up on the screen. She stared at it for a long moment, unwilling to deal with him. After several rings she muted the phone and stuck it back inside her purse.

Silence followed, and she exhaled, unaware until then that she'd been holding her breath. Her palms hurt, and she turned her hand over and saw that her long nails had made deep indentations in the sensitive skin of her palm.

For weeks she'd tried to convince herself that Cooper wasn't ashamed to be seen with her, but the love she felt had blinded her to the truth. Even what Claudia had explained to her over lunch couldn't refute the fact that he hadn't invited her to the dinner party.

Twenty minutes later the doorbell chimed.

"Ashley!" Cooper shouted and pounded on the door. "At least let me explain."

What could he possibly say that hadn't already been said more clearly by his action?

Her heart was crying out, demanding that she listen, but she'd been foolish in the past and had learned from her mistakes. She'd been too easily swayed by her love, but not again.

"Please don't do this," he said.

Her resolve weakened. Cooper had never sounded more sincere. She jerked open the hall closet door and whipped her faux fur jacket off the hanger, put it on and zipped it up all the way to her neck. Then she threw open the front door, crossed her arms and stared at a shocked Cooper with defiance flashing from her blue eyes.

"You have three minutes." Unable to look at him, she held up her wrist and pretended an acute interest in her watch.

"Where are you going?" he demanded.

"Two minutes and fifty seconds," she answered stiffly. "But if you must know, I'm going to see Webber. He happens to like me. It doesn't matter to him that my mother's some rich man's cook, or that my father's a laborer."

"It's Webb."

"Dear heaven," she said, and laughed almost hysterically. "You've got me doing it now."

"Ashley," he said, his voice softening. "It doesn't matter to me who your mother is or where your father works. I'm sorry about the party. I wouldn't want to hurt you for the world."

She bit into the soft skin of her inner lip to keep from letting herself be affected by his words. Her back rigid, she glared at the face of the watch, her body frozen. "Two minutes even," she murmured.

"I didn't think you'd want to come," he began again. "Mostly it's business associates —"

"Don't make excuses. I understand, believe me," she interrupted.

"I'm sure you don't," he countered sharply.

"But I do. I'm the kind of girl who enjoys pizza on the floor in front of a fireplace. I wouldn't fit in, that's what you're saying isn't it? It would be terribly embarrassing for all involved if I showed up wearing red cowboy boots. I might even break a piece of china or, worse yet, use the wrong spoon. No, I understand. I understand all too well." Her eyes and throat burned with the effort of suppressing tears. "Your time's up. Now, if you'll excuse me . . ." She stepped outside and closed the door.

"I want you to be there tomorrow night," he told her as she turned her key in the lock.

"I don't see any reason to make an issue over it. I couldn't have come anyway, I'm working tomorrow night."

"That's not true," he said harshly.

"You don't stop, do you? Does it give you pleasure to say these things to me . . . to call me a liar?" she whispered. "I suppose I should have learned how stubborn you are when I was forced to accept the car." She turned her stricken eyes to his. "I'm not lying."

"You told me school's out," he said with calculated anger.

"It is," she said. "This is my second job, the menial one. I'm a waitress, remember?"

Frustration marked his features as he followed her into the parking lot. "Ashley . . ."

"I'd like to stay and chat, but I have to be on my way." She paused and laughed mirthlessly. "I appreciate what you're trying to do, but you're the last person on God's green earth I ever want to see again. Goodbye, Cooper."

"Try to understand." The glimpse of pain she witnessed in his eyes couldn't be disguised. Despite what he'd done, she hadn't meant to hurt him, but in her own anguish she had lashed back at him. It was better that she leave now, before they said more hurtful things to one another.

A tight smile lingered on her mouth as she stared into his hard features. "I do understand," she whispered in defeat.

"I doubt that," he mumbled, as he opened the car door for her and stepped back.

She could see him in the side mirror,

standing stiff and proud, his look angry, arrogant. He almost fooled her, until he lifted a hand and wiped it across his face. When he dropped his arm, she noted the pain and frustration that glittered from his eyes. The sight made her ache inside, but she wouldn't let herself be influenced, not after what he'd done.

Ashley pulled out of the parking lot, intent on doing as she'd said. Webb would know what to say to comfort her. He was her friend, and she needed him. Tears blinded her vision, and she had to wipe them aside at every traffic signal. Tears would shock Webb; he'd never seen her cry.

Webb's car was in the driveway as she pulled in. He must have seen her arrive, because he opened the front door before she'd had time to ring the bell.

"Ashley." He sounded surprised, but his amazement quickly turned to apprehension. "Are you all right? You look upset. You're not crying, are you?"

All she could do was nod. "Oh, Webb," she sobbed, and walked into his arms.

He hugged her and patted her back like a comforting big brother, which was just what she needed. "I don't suppose this has anything to do with that Cooper character, does it?"

Miserably, she nodded. "How'd you know?"

He led her into the house and closed the door. "Because he just pulled up and parked across the street."

Ashley's head snapped up. "You're kidding! You mean he followed me here?" She took a tissue from her purse and blew her nose. "He probably followed me to find out if I was telling the truth."

"The truth?"

"I told him I was coming to see you. Do you mind?" She glanced up at him anxiously.

"Of course I don't mind." Webb's enthusiasm sounded forced. "Cooper's only four inches taller than I am and outweighs me by fifty pounds. Do you think he'll give me a choice of weapons?"

"You're being silly." She laughed, and then, to her supreme embarrassment, she hiccupped.

"Hang on," he said, and disappeared into the kitchen. A moment later he was back. "Here, drink this." He handed her a bottle of water.

She accepted because it gave her something to do with her hands. Tipping her head back, she took a large swallow.

"You're in love with him, aren't you?"

"Don't be ridiculous. I thoroughly dislike the man," she countered quickly.

"Now that's a sure sign. I wasn't positive before, but that clinched it."

"Webb, don't tease," she pleaded.

"Who's joking?" He led her to a chair, then sat across the room from her. "I've seen it coming on for the last couple of weeks. Other than the fact that he thinks I'm his arch rival and can't seem to get my name right, I like your Cooper."

"He's not mine," she said, more forcefully than she'd meant to.

"Okay, I won't argue. But if you love each other and really want things to work out, then whatever's wrong can be cleared up. If it doesn't, then you have to believe God has other plans for you."

Ashley closed her eyes for a long moment, then opened them and released a weary sigh. "You know, one of the worst things about you is that you're so darn logical. I can't stand it. I've always said an organized desk is the sign of a sick mind."

"And that, my friend, is one of the nicest things you've ever said to me."

They talked for a bit longer, and Webb did his best to raise her spirits. He joked with her, coaxing her to smile. Later they ordered pizza and played a game of

184

Scrabble. He won royally and refused to discount the fact that her mind wasn't on the game. When he walked her to the car, he kissed her lightly and waved as she backed out of the driveway.

Ashley slept fitfully, her heart heavy. The alarm went off at four-thirty, and she doubted that she'd gotten any rest. Cold water took the sleep out of her eyes, but she looked wan and felt worse. Connecting with the early ferry still meant a five-hour ride across Puget Sound to Victoria, British Columbia. The schedule gave her an hour to locate the antique shop, buy the saucer and connect with the ferry home. The trip would be tiring, and she would barely have enough time to shower and change clothes before leaving for her job at Lindo's Mexican Restaurant.

She had visited the Victorian seaport many times, and its beauty had never failed to enthrall her. Usually she came in summer when the Butchart Gardens were in full bloom. She found it amazing how a city tucked in the corner of the Pacific Northwest could have the feel, the flavor and the flair of England. Even the accent was decidedly British.

Without difficulty she located the small

antique shop off one of the many side streets that catered to the tourists. When Larry Marshall phoned she'd been so pleased to have found the saucer that she'd forgotten to ask about the price. She paled visibly when the proprietor cheerfully informed her how fortunate she was to have found this rare piece and she read the sticker. Her mind balked, but her pride made two hundred dollars for one small saucer sound like a bargain.

On the return trip, she stood at the rail. A demon wind whipped her hair across her face and numbed her with its cold. But she didn't leave, her eyes following the narrow strip of land until it gradually disappeared. Only when a freezing rain began to pelt the deck did she move inside. Surprisingly, she fell asleep until the foghorn blast of the ferry woke her as they eased into the dock in Seattle.

An hour later she smiled at Manuel, Lindo's manager, as she stepped in the back door. After hanging her coat on a hook in the kitchen, she paused long enough to tie an apron around her waist.

"There's someone to see you," Manuel told her in a heavy Spanish accent.

She looked up, perplexed.

"Out front," he added.

She peered around the corner to see a stern-faced Cooper sitting alone at a table. His steel-hard eyes met and trapped her as effectively as a vice.

CHAPTER 9

Carrying ice water and the menu, Ashley approached Cooper. What was he doing here? What about the party?

Dark, angry sparks flashed from his gaze, and a muscle twitched along the side of his jaw as his eyes followed her. "Where have you been all day?" he asked coldly.

Ashley ignored the question. "The daily special is chili verde." She pointed it out on the menu with the tip of her pencil. "I'll be back to take your order in a few minutes." Her voice contained a breathless tremor that betrayed what seeing him was doing to her. She hated herself for the weakness.

"Don't walk away from me," he warned. The lack of emotion in his voice was almost frightening.

"Are you ready to order now?" She took out the small pad from the apron pocket. Her fingers trembled slightly as she paused, ready to write down his choice.

"Ashley." His look was tight and grim. "Where were you?"

"I could say I was with Webb," she said, and swallowed tightly at the implication she was trying to give.

"Then you'd be lying," he added flatly.

"Yes, I would."

"Okay, we'll do this your way. It doesn't matter where you were or what sick game you've been playing with me. . . ."

"Sick game?" she echoed, remarkably calm. A sad smile touched her mouth as she averted her gaze.

"I didn't mean that," he muttered.

"It doesn't matter." She lowered her chin. "You'd think by now that we could accept the fact that we're wrong for one another. Forcing the issue is only going to hurt us." She paused and swallowed past the growing tightness in her throat. "I'm not willing to be hurt anymore."

His narrowed eyes searched hers. "I want you to come to the party with me."

Sadly, she hung her head. "No."

"I've already talked to the manager. He says he doesn't think tonight's going to be all that busy anyway."

"I won't go," she repeated insistently.

"Then I'm not leaving. I'll sit here all night if that's what it takes." The tight set of his mouth convinced her the threat wasn't idle.

"But you can't, your guests . . ." She stopped, angry at how easily she'd fallen into his plan. "I won't be blackmailed, Cooper. Sit here all night if you like." Her pulse raced wildly.

"All right." His head shifted slightly to one side as he studied the menu. "I'll take a plate of nachos and the special you mentioned."

Furiously, she wrote down the order.

"You stay?" Manuel asked after she called Cooper's order into the kitchen. "I already call my cousin to come in and work for you. You can go to this important party."

"I'm here to work, Manuel," she explained in a patient tone. "I'm sure there will be enough work for both your cousin and me."

Nothing seemed to be going right. Cooper watched her every action like a hawk studying its prey before the kill. By seven o'clock Manuel's cousin had served nearly every customer. Only two customers were seated in her section. Ashley was convinced Cooper had somehow arranged that. She wanted to cry in frustration.

"Cooper," she pleaded, "won't you please leave? It's almost seven."

"I won't go without you," he told her calmly.

"Talk about sick games," she lashed back, and to her consternation a sensuous smile curved his mouth.

"I'm not playing games," he stated firmly.

"Then if you miss your own party it's your problem." She tried to sound nonchalant.

By seven-fifteen she was pacing the floor, her resolve weakening. Cooper couldn't offend his associates this way. It could hurt him and his business.

Using the need to refill his coffee cup as an excuse, she avoided his gaze as she said, "I don't have anything to wear."

"Cowboy boots are fine. I'll wear mine, if you like." Her hand was suddenly captured between his. "Nothing in the world means more to me than having you at my side tonight."

"Oh, Cooper," she moaned. "I don't know. I don't belong there."

He studied her slowly, his eyes focused on her soft mouth. "You belong with me."

She felt the determination to defy him drain out of her. "All right," she whispered in defeat.

"Thank God." As he hurried out of the booth he added, "I'll meet you at your place."

Numbly she nodded. As it worked out, he pulled into the apartment parking lot directly behind her.

"While you change, I'll phone Claudia."

Ashley wanted to kick herself for being so weak. Examining the contents of her closet, she pulled out a wool blend dress with a Victorian flair. The antique lace inserts around the neck, bodice and cuffs gave the white dress a formal look. The glittering gold belt matched the high heels she chose.

Her fingers shook as she applied a light layer of makeup. After a moment of hurried effort, she gripped the edge of the small bathroom sink as she stopped to pray. It wasn't the first time today that she'd turned to God. She'd tried to pray standing on the deck of the ferry, the wind whipping at her, but somehow the words wouldn't come. The pain of Cooper's rejection had been too sharp to voice, even to God. Now, having finished, she lifted her head and released a shuddering breath. More confident, she added a dab of perfume to the pulse points at her wrists and neck, and stepped out to meet Cooper.

He turned around as she entered the room. A shocked look entered his eyes. "You're beautiful."

"Don't sound so surprised. I can dress up

every now and then."

"You're a little pale. Come here, I can change that." Before she was aware of what he was doing, he pulled her into his arms and kissed her. The demand of his mouth tilted her head back. His hand pressed against her back, arching her against him.

Ashley's breath caught in her lungs at the unexpectedness of his action. Her hands were poised on the broad expanse of his chest, his heartbeat hammering against her palm.

"There." He tilted his face to study her. "Plenty of color now." Releasing her, he held her coat open so she could easily slip her arms inside. "I'm afraid we're going to make something of a grand entrance. Everyone's arrived. Claudia sounded frantic. She said the hors d'oeuvres ran out fifteen minutes ago."

"Is my mother . . . ?" She let the rest of the question fade, sure Cooper would know what she was asking.

"No, it's being catered." With a hand at the back of her waist, he urged her out the door.

"Oh, Cooper." She hurried back inside. "I almost forgot." Her heels made funny little noises against the floor as she rushed into her bedroom and came out with the wrapped package. "Here." She gave it to him.

"Do I have to wait for Christmas?"

"No. It's a replacement for the saucer I broke, the one from your grandmother's service."

"I can't believe . . . Where did you ever find it?"

"Don't ask."

"Ashley . . ." He set his hands on her shoulders and turned her around so she was facing him. "Is this what you were up to today?"

She nodded silently.

His mouth thinned as his look became distant. "I think I went a little crazy looking for you." He slipped an arm around her waist. "We'll talk about that later. If we keep Claudia waiting another minute, she's likely to disown us both."

The street and driveway outside Cooper's house looked like a high performance car showroom. Ashley felt her nerves tense as she clenched her hands in her lap.

"Ashley, stop."

"Stop?"

"I can feel you tightening up like a coiled spring. Every man here is going to be envious of me. Just be yourself."

The front door flew open before they were

194

halfway up the walk. Claudia stood there like an avenging warlord, waving her arms and glaring at them.

"Thank goodness you're here!" she exclaimed forcefully. "If you ever do this to me again, I swear I'll . . ." Her voice drifted away. "Don't stand out here listening to me, get inside. Everyone's waiting." Her gaze narrowed on Cooper. "And I do mean everyone."

Ashley didn't need to be reminded that some of the most important people in Seattle would be there.

Claudia gave her an encouraging smile, winked and took her coat.

His hand at her elbow, Cooper led Ashley into the living room. The low conversational hum rose as a few guests called out his name. Apparently the champagne had been flowing freely, because no one seemed to mind that Cooper was late to his own party.

He introduced her to several couples, though she knew she couldn't hope to remember all the names. After twenty minutes the smile felt frozen on her face. Someone handed her a glass of what she assumed was wine, but she didn't drink it. Tonight she would need to keep her wits about her in a room full of intimidating people. There was hardly room to maneuver, and she felt as if the walls were closing in around her.

"Is this the little lady who kept us waiting?" A distinguished, middle-aged man with silver streaks at his temples asked Cooper for an introduction.

"I am," she admitted with a weak smile. "I hope you'll forgive me."

"I find it very easy to forgive someone as pretty as you. Maybe we could get together later, so I can listen to your excuse."

"Whoa, Tom," Cooper teased, but his voice contained an underlying warning. "The lady's with me."

With a good-natured chuckle, Tom slapped him across the shoulder. "Anything you say."

Ashley spotted Claudia at the far side of the room. "If you'll both excuse me a minute . . . ?" she whispered.

Claudia caught her eye and arched her delicate brows.

"Boy, am I glad to see a familiar face," Ashley said, and released a slow sigh as she leaned against the wall for support.

"What took you two so long?" Claudia demanded. "I was frantic. You wouldn't believe some of the excuses I gave. Dear heavens, Ash, where were you today? I thought Cooper was going to go mad."

"Canada."

"Canada?" Claudia shot back. "Well, I must admit, that was one place he didn't look. Have you talked to your mother yet? I don't know what he said to her, but he was closed up in his den for an hour afterward. Believe me, he didn't look happy. No one, not even the boys, could get near him."

"I know he feels miserable about the whole thing, but I understand better than he realizes. I wouldn't have invited me to this party, either. Look at me. I stick out like a sore thumb."

"If you do, it's because you're the prettiest woman here."

Ashley's light laugh was forced. "You're a better friend than I thought."

"I *am* your friend, but don't underestimate yourself." A hush came over the room as someone in a caterer's apron made the announcement that dinner was ready. "I don't know why Cooper wouldn't invite you tonight. He wasn't overly pleased with me for letting the cat out of the bag, I can tell you that."

"No, I imagine he wasn't." How much simpler things would have been if she'd stayed innocently unaware. "But I'm glad you did," she murmured, and hung her head. "Very glad." When she glanced up she saw the object of their conversation weaving his way toward her. Progress was slow, as people stopped to chat or ask him a question. Although he smiled and chatted, his probing gaze didn't leave her for more than a moment.

"I don't want you hiding in a corner," he muttered when he finally got to her, and gripped her elbow, then led her toward the huge dining room.

"I'm not hiding," she defended herself. "I just wanted to talk to Claudia for a minute."

"It was far longer than a minute," he said between clenched teeth.

"Honestly, Cooper, are you going to start an argument now? I'm here under protest as it is."

"You're here because I want you here. It's where you belong." His control over his temper seemed fragile.

Rather than say anything she would regret later, Ashley pinched her mouth tightly closed.

The dining room table had been extended to accommodate forty guests. Ashley looked at the china and sparkling crystal, and the fir and candle centerpiece that extended the full length of the table. Everything was exquisite, and she was filled with a sense of awe. She didn't belong here. What was she doing fooling herself?

Cooper sat at the head of the table, with Ashley at his right side. Under normal circumstances she would have enjoyed the meal. The caterers had also supplied four waitresses, and she found herself watching their movements instead of involving herself in idle conversation with Cooper or the white-haired man on her right. Once the salad plates were removed, they were served prime rib, fresh green beans and new potatoes. Every bite and swallow was calculated, measured, to be sure she would do nothing that would call attention to herself. For dessert a cake in the shape of a yule log was carried into the room. She only took one bite, afraid she would end up spilling frosting on her white dress. Once, when she glanced up, she found Cooper watching her, his look both foreboding and thoughtful. If this was a test, she was certain she was failing miserably, and his look did nothing to boost her confidence.

When the meal was finished, she couldn't recall ever being more relieved.

Cooper's hand was pressed to her waist, keeping her at his side, as they moved into the living room. She didn't join the conversation, only smiled and nodded at the appropriate times. An hour later, her face felt frozen into a permanent smile.

A few people started to leave. Grateful for the opportunity to slip away, she murmured a friendly farewell and left Cooper to deal with his guests.

"I don't know how much more of this I can take," she whispered to Claudia.

"Don't worry, you're doing great. Not much longer now."

"Where's Seth?"

"Checking the boys. He's not much for this kind of thing, either. Haven't you noticed the way he keeps loosening his tie? By the time the evening's over, the whole thing will be missing."

"What time is it?" Ashley muttered.

"Just after eleven."

"How much longer?"

"I don't know. Don't look now, but Cooper's headed our way."

His stern expression hadn't relaxed. He was obviously displeased about something. "I want to talk to you in my den when everyone's gone." His look was ominous as he turned and left.

Primly, Ashley clasped her hands together in front of her. "Heavens, what did I do now?" she asked Claudia.

Claudia shrugged. "I don't know, but for heaven's sake, humor him. Another day like today, and Seth and I are packing our bags and finding a hotel."

By the time the last couple had left, Ashley's stomach was coiled into a hard lump.

The caterers were clearing away glasses and the last of the dishes from the living room when Cooper found her in the corner talking to Seth and Claudia. As Claudia had predicted, Seth's tie had mysteriously disappeared. His arm was draped across his wife's shoulders.

Seth looked over to Cooper. "You don't mind if we head upstairs, do you?"

"No, no, go ahead." Cooper's answer sounded pre-occupied. He gestured toward his den. "We'll be more comfortable in there," he said to Ashley.

She tossed Claudia a puzzled look. Cooper didn't look upset anymore, and she didn't know what to think. His face was tight and drawn, but not with anger. She couldn't recall ever seeing him quite like this.

"Oh!" Claudia paused halfway up the stairs and turned around. "Don't forget tomorrow morning. We'll pick you up around ten. The boys are looking forward to it."

"I am, too," Ashley replied.

They entered the familiar den, and he

closed the door, leaning against the heavy wood momentarily. He gestured toward a chair, and she sat down, her back straight.

Again he paused. He rubbed the back of his neck, and when he glanced up, it struck Ashley that she couldn't remember ever having seen him look more tired.

"Cooper, are you feeling all right? You're not sick, are you?"

"Sick?" he repeated slowly. "No."

"What's wrong, then? You look like you've lost your best friend."

"In some ways, I think I have." He moved across the room to his desk, rearranging the few items that littered the top.

Impatiently, Ashley watched him. He'd said he wanted to talk to her, yet he seemed hesitant.

"How do you feel about the way things went tonight?" he asked finally.

"What do you mean? Was the food good? It was excellent. Do I like your friends? I found them to be cordial, if a bit overwhelming. Cooper, you have to remember I'm just an ordinary schoolteacher."

The pencil he'd just picked up snapped in two. "You know, I think I'm sick of hearing how ordinary you are."

"What do you mean?" She watched as his mouth formed a brittle line.

"You ran to a corner to hide every chance you got. You wouldn't so much as lift a fork until you'd examined the way three other people were holding theirs to be sure you did it the same way."

"Is that so bad?" she flared. "I felt safe in a corner."

"And not with me?"

"No!"

"I think that tells me everything I want to know."

"You forced me into coming tonight," she accused him.

"It was a no-win situation. You understand that, don't you?"

She stood and moved to the far side of the room. Cooper was talking down to her as if she was a disobedient child, and she hated it. "No, I don't. But there's very little I understand about you anymore."

"I didn't invite you tonight for a reason!" he shouted.

"Do you think I don't already know that?" she flashed bitterly. "I don't fit in with this crowd."

"That's not why," he insisted loudly.

"If you raise your voice to me one more time, I'm leaving." Tears welled in her eyes. How she hated to cry. Her eyes stung, and her throat ached. "It's not the first time, either, is it?"

"What are you talking about?" He tossed her a puzzled look.

"For a while I thought it was just my overactive imagination. That I was thinking like an insecure schoolgirl. But it's true."

"What are you talking about?" What little patience he had was quickly evaporating.

"The first time we went out, you chose a small Italian restaurant, and I thought you didn't want to be seen with me."

"You can't honestly believe that?" His eyes filled with disbelief.

"Then Claudia phoned on Thanksgiving Day and I was there, but you didn't say a word." She paused long enough to swallow back a sob. "I knew you didn't want Claudia or Seth or anyone else to know I was with you. Even in church when you held my hand, it was done secretively and only when there wasn't a possibility of anyone seeing us."

A tense silence enclosed them.

"You've thought that all this time?" The dark, troubled look was back on his face.

She nodded. "I don't know about you, but I'm tired. I want to go home."

His dark eyes searched her face. She noted the weariness that wrinkled his brow and the indomitable pride in his stern jaw.

He opened the door wordlessly and re-trieved her coat. He didn't say a word until he pulled up in front of her apartment building. "I find it amazing that you could think all those things, yet continue to see me."

"Now that you mention it, so do I," she returned bitterly.

His mouth thinned, but he didn't retali-ate.

She handed him her apartment key, and he unlocked the door. She held out her hand, waiting for him to return the key. He didn't seem to notice, his look a thousand miles away.

When he did glance up, their eyes met and held. The troubled look remained, but with flecks of something she couldn't quite decipher. A softness entered as he lowered his gaze to her soft mouth. "It's not true, Ashley, none of it." With that he turned and left.

Stunned, she stood watching him until he was out of sight.

Her room was dark and still when she turned out the light. She hadn't behaved well tonight. That was what had originally upset Cooper. But she'd been frightened, out of her element. Those people were important, and she was nothing. The four walls surrounding her seemed to close in. Why had he left that way? For once, couldn't he have stayed and explained himself? Tomorrow she would make sure everything was cleared up between them. No more misunderstandings, her heart couldn't take it.

"Are you ready, Auntie Ash?" Johnny asked as he bounded into her apartment excitedly the next morning.

"You bet." She bent over to give her godson a big hug.

"You should hurry, cause Daddy's driving Uncle Cooper's car," John added.

Ashley straightened. "Where's Cooper?"

"He decided at the last minute not to come. What happened with you two last night?" Claudia asked.

"Why?"

Claudia glanced at her son, who was impatiently pacing the floor. "We'll talk about it later."

"Uncle Cooper bought the car seat just for Scotty," Johnny told her proudly when she climbed in the back seat. "He said I was a big boy and could use a special one with a real seat belt. Watch." He pulled the belt across his small body, and after several tries the lock clicked into place. "See? I can do it all by myself."

"Good for you." Ashley looped an arm around his shoulders.

"You should put yours on, too," Johnny insisted. "Uncle Cooper does."

"I think you're right," she agreed with a wry smile.

It was all Ashley could do not to quiz her friend about Cooper's absence as Seth maneuvered in and out of the heavy traffic.

"Christmas Eve Day," Johnny said as he looked around eagerly. "It's Jesus's birthday tomorrow, and we get to open all our gifts. Scotty's never opened presents."

"I don't think he'll have any problem getting the hang of it," Seth teased from the front seat.

"You're coming tonight, aren't you, Ash?" Claudia half turned to glance into the rear seat.

"I don't know," Ashley said, trying to ignore the heaviness that weighted her heart.

"But I thought it was already settled. Christmas Eve with us and Christmas with your parents."

Ashley pretended an inordinate amount of interest in the scenery flashing past outside her window. "I thought it was, too." Cooper was saying several things with his absence today. One of them was crystal clear. "Maybe I'll come for a little while. I want to see the boys open the presents from Cooper and me."

"Do I get to open a present tonight?" Johnny demanded.

Claudia threw Ashley a disgruntled look. "We'll see," she answered her son.

The downtown Seattle area was crowded with last minute shoppers. Amazingly, Seth found a parking place on the street. While Ashley and Claudia dug through the bottoms of their purses for the correct change for the meter, Seth opened the trunk and retrieved the stroller for Scotty.

"Can I put the money in?" Johnny wanted to know.

Ashley handed him the coins and lifted him up so he could insert them into the slot.

"Good boy," Ashley said, and he beamed proudly.

"Now tell me what happened," Claudia insisted in a low voice. "I'm dying to know."

"Nothing, really. He wasn't pleased with the way the party turned out. Mainly, he was disappointed in me."

"In *you*?" Claudia looked surprised. "What did you do? I thought you were fine."

"I don't understand him, Claudia." She couldn't conceal a sigh of regret. "First, he pointedly doesn't invite me and openly admits he didn't want me there. Then he forcefully insists that I attend. And to make matters worse, he doesn't approve of the way I acted."

"If you ask me, I think he's got a lot of nerve," Claudia admitted. "I hardly spoke to him this morning. But something's wrong. He's miserable. He loves you, I'd bet my life on it. It would be a terrible shame if you two didn't get together."

"I suppose."

"You suppose?" Claudia drawled the word slowly. "If you love one another, then nothing should keep you apart."

"Spoken like a true optimist. But I'm not right for Cooper," Ashley announced sadly. "He needs someone with a little more — I hate to use this word, but . . . finesse."

"And you need someone more easy-going and fun-loving. Like Webb," Claudia finished for her.

"No, not at all." Ashley's cool blue eyes turned questioningly toward her friend. "I'm surprised you'd even suggest that. Webb's a friend, nothing more."

Clearly pleased, Claudia shook her head knowingly. "I don't think you realize that you bring out the best in Cooper, or that he does the same for you. I don't think I've seen a couple who belong together more than you two."

"Oh, Claudia, I hope we do, because I love him so much."

"Have you ever thought about letting *him* know that?"

A blustery wind whipped Ashley's coat around her, preventing her from answering.

"I think we should catch the monorail," Seth suggested. "It's getting windy out here. Agreed?"

The two women had been so caught up in their conversation they'd hardly noticed.

"Fine." Ashley shook her head.

"Sure," Claudia said, looking a little guilty as Seth handled both boys so she could talk.

For a nominal fee they were able to catch the transport that had been built as part of the Seattle World's Fair in 1962. The rail delivered them to the heart of the Seattle Center, only a few blocks from the Food Circus.

The boys squealed with delight the minute they spied the Enchanted Forest. Scotty clapped his hands gleefully and pointed to the kiddy size train that traveled between artificial trees.

"Are you hungry?" Seth wanted to know.

"Not me." Ashley's thoughts were on other things.

"I wouldn't object to cotton candy,"

Claudia confessed.

"I had to ask," Seth teased, and lovingly brushed his lips over his wife's cheek.

Ashley viewed the tender scene with building despair. Someday, she wanted Cooper to look at her like that. More than anything else, she wanted to share her life with him, have his children.

"Ash, are you all right?" Claudia asked.

Quickly, she shook her head. "Of course. What made you ask?"

"You looked so sad."

"I am, I . . ."

"My goodness, Ash, look, Cooper's here."

"Cooper?" Her spirits soared. "Where?"

"Across the room." Claudia pointed, then waved when he saw them.

His level gaze crossed the crowded room to hold Ashley's, his look discouraging.

"I'm going to do it," Ashley said, straightening. Claudia gave her a funny look, but didn't question her as she started toward him.

They met halfway. He looked tired, but just as determined as she felt.

"Ashley."

"I want to talk to you," she said sternly.

"I want to talk to *you,* too."

"Wonderful. Let me go first."

He looked at her blankly. "All right," he agreed.

"You asked me last night why I continued to see you if I believed all those things I confessed. I'll tell you why. Simply. Honestly. I love you, Cooper Masters, and if you don't love me, I think I'll die."

CHAPTER 10

"That's not the kind of thing you say to a man in a public place." He studied her face for a tantalizing moment, gradually softening.

"I know, and I apologize, but I couldn't hold it in any longer."

"Why couldn't you have told me that last night?"

Oblivious to the crowds milling around, they stared at one another with only a small space separating them.

"Because I was afraid, and you were so . . ."

Cooper rubbed a hand across his eyes. "Don't say it. I know how I was."

"When you weren't with Claudia this morning, I didn't know what to think."

"I couldn't come. Not when you believed that I didn't want to be seen with you — that I was ashamed of you. You've carried that inside all these weeks, and not once did

213

you question me."

Her teeth bit tightly into her lower lip. "I was afraid. Sounds silly, doesn't it?" She didn't wait for him to answer. "Afraid if I brought my fears into the open and forced you to admit it, that I wouldn't see you again. I couldn't face the truth if it meant losing you."

"The day you started ranting about your mother being my cook and your father being a steelworker . . . Was that the reason?"

She looked away and nodded.

Slowly he shook his head. "I can understand how you came to that conclusion, but you couldn't be more wrong. I love you, Ashley, I —"

"Cooper, oh, Cooper," she cried excitedly and threw her arms around him, spreading happy kisses over his face.

His mouth intercepted her as he hungrily devoured her lips. Although she could hear the people around them, she wouldn't have cared if they were in New York City at Grand Central Station. Cooper loved her. She'd prayed to hear those words, and nothing, not even a Christmas crowd in a public place, was going to ruin her pleasure.

When he dragged his mouth from hers, his husky voice breathed against her ear, "Do you promise to do that every time I admit I love you."

"Yes, oh, yes," she said with a joyous smile.

He cleared his throat self-consciously. "In case you hadn't noticed, we have an audience."

She was too contented to care. A searing happiness was bubbling within her. "I want the whole world to know how I feel."

"You seem to have gotten a good start," he teased with an easy laugh, and kissed the top of her head. "Don't look now, but Claudia and company are headed our way."

Reluctantly, Ashley dropped her arms and stepped back. Cooper pulled her close to his side, cradling her waist.

"Is everything okay with you two, or do you need more time?" Claudia's gaze went from one of them to the other. "If that embrace was anything to go by, I'd say things are looking much better."

"You could say that," Cooper agreed, his eyes holding Ashley's. The look he gave her was so warm and loving that it seemed to burst free and touch her heart and soul.

"But there are several things we need to discuss," Cooper continued. "If you don't mind, I'm going to take Ashley with me. We'll all meet back at the house later."

Claudia and Seth exchanged knowing

looks. "We don't mind," Seth answered for them.

"But . . . Seth has your car," Ashley said, confused. "How will we . . . ?"

He smiled. "I have a second car, since I can't afford to be without transportation. We'll be fine."

"Do I still get to open a present tonight? Because Auntie Ash said we could," Johnny quizzed anxiously, not the least bit interested in the logistics of the grown-ups' plans.

Cooper's eyes met Claudia's, and she shrugged.

"I think that will be fine, if that's what your Auntie Ash said," Seth interrupted.

"Uncle Cooper?" John's head tilted up at an inquiring angle.

"Yes?" He squatted down so that he was eye level with his godson.

"Is there mistletoe here, too?"

Briefly Cooper scanned the interior of the huge building. "I don't see any, why?"

"Cause you were kissing Auntie Ash again."

"Sometime I like to kiss her even when there isn't any reason."

"You mean like Daddy and Mommy?"

"Exactly," he said, and smiled as his eyes caught Ashley's.

"I think it's time we left and let these two talk. We'll meet you later," Seth announced. Claudia lifted Johnny into her arms and turned around, then looked back and winked.

"Are you hungry?" Cooper asked.

She hadn't eaten all day. "Starved. I hardly touched dinner last night."

"I noticed." His tone was dry.

She ignored it. "And then this morning I was too miserable to think about food. But now I could eat a cow."

"We're at the right place. Choose what you want, and while you find us a table, I'll go get it."

The Food Circus had a large variety of booths that sold every imaginable cuisine. The toughest decision was making a choice from everything that was available.

They hardly spoke as they ate their chicken. Ashley licked her fingers. Cooper carefully unfolded one of the moistened towelettes that had been provided with their meal and carefully cleaned his own hands.

He glanced up and found her watching him. A tiny smile twitched at the corner of her mouth. "What's so funny?" he asked.

"Us." She opened her own towelette and followed his example. "Claudia told me she didn't know any two people more meant for one another."

Cooper acknowledged the statement with a curt nod. "I know I love you, whether we're right or wrong for one another doesn't seem to be the question." He reached across the table and captured her hand. "But then, you're an easy person to love. You're warm and alive, and so unique you make my heart sing just watching you."

"And you're so calm and dignified. Nothing rattles you, and so many times I've wished I could be like that."

"We balance one another." His eyes searched hers in a room that seemed filled with only them.

A burst of applause diverted Cooper's attention to the antics of a clown. "Let's get out of here."

Ashley happily agreed.

They stood, dumped their garbage in the proper receptacles, and linked their arms around one another's waists as they strolled outside.

A chill raced over her forearms, and she shivered.

Cooper brought her closer to his side. "Cold?"

"Only when you close me out," she whispered truthfully. "If you hadn't admitted to loving me, I don't know that I could have withstood the cold."

He drank deeply from her eyes, perhaps realizing for the first time how strong her emotions rang. "We need to talk," he murmured, and quickened his pace.

A half hour later he pulled into the driveway of his home.

"Coffee?" he suggested as he hung her coat in the hall closet.

"Yes." She nodded eagerly. "But, Cooper, could I have it in a mug? I'd feel safer."

His mouth thinned slightly, and she knew her request had troubled him. "I'm not the dainty teacup type," she said more forcefully than she wanted to. "What I mean is . . ."

"I know what you mean." Lightly he pressed a kiss on her cheek, then against the hollow of her throat. "Do you have any idea how difficult it's been this week to keep my hands off you?"

"Not half as difficult as it's been not to encourage you to touch me," she admitted, and felt color suffuse her cheeks.

A few minutes later he carried two ceramic mugs into the den on a silver platter.

A soft smile danced from Ashley's eyes. "Compromise?"

"Compromise," he agreed, handing her one of the mugs.

She held it with both hands and stared into its depths. "I have a feeling I know what you're going to say."

"I doubt that very much, but go ahead."

"No." She shook her head, then nervously tugged a strand of hair around her ear. "I've put my foot in my mouth so many times that for once I'm content to let you do the talking."

"We seem to have a penchant for saying the wrong things to each other, don't we?" His gaze searched hers, and the silence was broken only by an occasional snap and pop from the logs in the fireplace.

His look was thoughtful as he straightened in his chair. Nervously, she glanced around the den she had come to love — the books and desk, the chess set. One of the most ostentatious rooms in the house and, strangely, the one in which she felt the most comfortable. Maybe it was because this was the room Cooper used most often.

"I think it's important to clear away any misunderstandings, especially about the party. Ashley, when I saw how hurt you were to be excluded, well . . . I can't remember ever feeling worse. Believe this, because it's the truth. I wanted you there from the first. But I felt you would be uncomfortable. Those people are a lot like me."

"But I love you," she said, keeping her gaze on her coffee.

"I didn't know that at the time. I didn't want to do anything that was going to make you feel ill-at-ease. Thrusting you into my world could have destroyed our promising relationship, and that was far more important to me. Now I realize what a terrible mistake that was."

"And the other things?" She had to know, had to clear away any reasons for doubt.

"Thinking over everything you've told me, your point of view makes perfect sense." He set his cup aside and sat on the ottoman in front of her chair. Holding her face with both hands, he tilted her gaze to meet his. Ashley couldn't doubt the sincerity of his look. "I did those things because I thought you wouldn't want to be associated with me. I didn't let Claudia know you were here on Thanksgiving when she phoned to protect you from speculation and embarrassing questions. The same with what happened in church."

"Oh, Cooper . . ." She groaned at her own stupidity. "I was so miserable. I know it was stupid not to say anything, but I was afraid of the truth."

His kiss was sweet and filled with the awe of the discovery of her love. "Things being what they are, maybe you should open your Christmas gift now."

"Oh, could I?"

"I think you'd better." He opened the closet and brought out a large, beautifully wrapped box.

Much bigger than an engagement ring, Ashley mused thoughtfully, fighting to overcome her disappointment. Cowboy boots? She'd tried on a couple of pairs when they'd bought his, but she'd decided against them because of the expense. But if her present was cowboy boots, why would Cooper feel it was important to give it to her now?

He placed it on her lap, and she untied the red velvet bow, then hesitated. "My gift to you is at home." It was important that he know he'd meant enough to her to buy him something special. "But I'm making you wait until Christmas."

"Maybe I should make *you* wait, too," he teased, ready to take back the gaily wrapped present.

"No you don't," she objected, and gripped the package tightly.

"Actually," he said, and the teasing light left his eyes, "it's important that you open this now." He smiled huskily and kissed her. His lips were a light caress across her brow.

Ashley's fingers shook as she pulled back the paper and lifted the lid of the box. Inside, nestled in white tissue, was a large family Bible. Her heart was thumping so loudly she could barely hear Cooper speaking above the hammering beat.

"A Bible," she murmured and looked up at him, her gaze probing his.

"I've thought about what you said about your relationship with Christ, and how important it was to you. I wanted to have a strong faith for you, because of my love. But that wasn't good enough. There were so many things I didn't understand. If Christ paid the price for my salvation with His life, then how can my faith be of value if all I have to do is ask for it?" He stood and walked across the room, pausing once to run his hand through his hair. "I talked to Seth about it several times. He always had the answers, but I wasn't convinced. Last Sunday I was in church, sitting in the sanctuary waiting for the service to begin, and I asked God to help me. On the way out of church after the service I saw the car I had given you in the parking lot. Suddenly I knew."

Ashley had been at church, but she had taught Sunday School and then helped in the nursery during the worship service. She had talked only briefly to Claudia and hadn't seen Cooper at all.

"My car? How did my car help?"

"It sounds crazy, I know," he admitted wryly. "But I gave it to you because I love you. Freely, without seeking reimbursement, knowing that you couldn't afford a car. It was my gift to you, because I love you. It suddenly occurred to me that was exactly why Christ died for me. He paid the price because I couldn't."

Unabashed tears of happiness clouded her eyes as her hands lovingly traced the gilded print on the cover of the Bible.

"I've made my commitment to Christ," he told her, his voice rich and vibrant. "He's my Savior."

"Oh, Cooper." She wiped a tear from her cheek and smiled up at him.

"That's not all."

An overwhelming happiness stole through her. She couldn't imagine anything more wonderful than what he'd just finished explaining.

"Do you recall the first Sunday Claudia and Seth arrived?"

Ashley nodded.

"I stepped into your Sunday school class." He looked away as a glossy shine came over his dark eyes. "You were on the floor with a little girl sitting in your lap."

"I remember. You turned around and walked out. I thought I'd done something to upset you."

"Upset me?" he repeated incredulously. "No. Never that. You looked up, and your blue eyes softened, and in that moment I imagined you holding another child. Ours. Never have I felt an emotion so strong. It nearly choked me, I could hardly think. If I hadn't turned around and walked away, I don't know what I would have done."

Ashley thought her heart would burst with unrestrained joy. "Our child."

"Yes." Cooper knelt on the floor beside her, took the Bible out of its box and set the box on the floor. Reverently, he opened the first pages of the holy book. "I got this one for a reason. I've written our names here, and I'm asking that we fill the rest out together."

Ashley looked down at the page, which had been set aside to record a family history. Both their names were entered under "Marriage," the date left blank.

"Will you marry me, Ashley?" he asked, an unfamiliar humble quality in his voice.

The lump of joy in her throat prevented her from doing anything but nodding her head. "Yes," she finally managed. "Yes,

Cooper, yes." She flung her arms around his neck and spread kisses over his face. She laughed with breathless joy as the tears slid down her cheeks.

His arms went around her as he pulled her closer. His mouth found hers in a lingering kiss that cast away all doubts and misgivings.

She lovingly caressed the side of his face. "I don't know how you can love me. I always seem to think the worst of you."

"Not anymore you won't," he whispered against her temple as he continued to stroke her back. "I won't ever give you reason to doubt again. I love you, Ashley."

She linked her hands behind his neck and smiled contentedly into his eyes. "I do want children. Just being with Johnny and Scott has shown me how much I want babies of my own."

"We'll fill the house. I can't wait to tuck them into bed at night and listen to their prayers."

"What about horsey rides?"

"Those too."

"Cooper . . ." She paused and swallowed tightly. "Why were you so angry with me after the party?" She wanted everything to be right and needed to know what she'd done to displease him.

Some of the happiness left his face. "I love you so much, Ashley. It hurt me to see you so uncomfortable, afraid to make a move. Your fun-loving, outgoing nature had been completely squelched. I wanted you to be yourself. Later —" He sat on the ottoman and took both her hands in his. "— I had already gotten the Bible with the hope of asking you to marry me, and you listed off all the things I had done to make you believe I was ashamed to be seen with you. I don't mind telling you that it shook me up. I was on the verge of asking you to be my wife, and you didn't even know how much I loved you."

"I won't have that problem again," she told him softly.

"I know you won't, because you'll never have reason to doubt again. I promise you that, my love."

The sound of footsteps in the hall brought their attention to the world outside the door.

Cooper stood, and extended a hand toward her. "I don't think either Claudia or Seth will be surprised by our announcement. Or your family, for that matter."

"My family?"

"I talked to your mother and father yesterday. They've given us their blessing. I was determined to have you, Ash. I wouldn't want to live my life without you now." He hugged her tightly and curved an arm around her waist. "Christmas. It's almost too wonderful to believe. God gave His Son in love. And now He's given me you."

ABOUT THE AUTHOR

Debbie Macomber is a number one *New York Times* and *USA TODAY* bestselling author. Her books include *1225 Christmas Tree Lane, 1105 Yakima Street, A Turn in the Road, Hannah's List* and *Debbie Macomber's Christmas Cookbook,* as well as *Twenty Wishes, Summer on Blossom Street* and *Call Me Mrs. Miracle.* She has become a leading voice in women's fiction worldwide and her work has appeared on every major bestseller list, including those of the *New York Times, USA TODAY, Publishers Weekly* and *Entertainment Weekly.* She is a multiple award winner, and won the 2005 Quill Award for Best Romance. There are more than 100 million copies of her books in print. Two of her Harlequin MIRA Christmas titles have been made into Hallmark Channel Original Movies, and the Hallmark Channel is launching a series based on her bestselling

Cedar Cove series. For more information on Debbie and her books, visit her website: www.DebbieMacomber.com.